W9-BFP-726

# Map of the
# IDITAROD TRAIL
# INTERNATIONAL SLED
# DOG RACE
from Anchorage to Nome

The Mapmakers, Palmer, Alaska

SOUTH HIGH COMMUNITY LIBRARY

# The Hour of the Wolf

*Also by Patricia Calvert*
THE SNOWBIRD
THE MONEY CREEK MARE
THE STONE PONY

# The
# HOUR
## of the
# WOLF

.:.

*Patricia Calvert*

CHARLES SCRIBNER'S SONS
NEW YORK

The author gratefully acknowledges the cooperation of
Joanne Potts, of the Iditarod Trail Committee,
and of Brigetta Lively,
who kindly supplied the map of the Iditarod Trail.

*Copyright © 1983 Patricia Calvert*

Library of Congress Cataloging in Publication Data
Calvert, Patricia.    The hour of the wolf.
Summary: Following his suicide attempt, a loner and
a loser who has never lived up to his father's expecta-
tions is sent to Alaska, where he subsequently enters
the annual thousand-mile-long Iditarod Trail Race from
Anchorage to Nome in memory of his Athabascan Indian
friend who dies.
[1. Suicide—Fiction.   2. Fathers and sons—Fiction.
3. Sled dog racing—Fiction.   4. Alaska—Fiction]
I. Title.
PZ7.C139Ho    1983    [Fic]    83-14184
ISBN 0-684-17961-X

This book published simultaneously in the
United States of America and in Canada—
Copyright under the Berne Convention.
All rights reserved. No part of this book
may be reproduced in any form without the
permission of Charles Scribner's Sons.

3 5 7 9 11 13 15 17 19  F/C  20 18 16 14 12 10 8 6 4 2

*Printed in the United States of America.*

*For*
*Jake and Katie,*
*with love*

I<small>N</small> <small>FORESTS</small> long ago there was a time between dusk and dawn when wolves and evil spirits were said to stalk the footsteps of unwary travelers. Such a time was aptly called *the hour of the wolf*. Do modern folk hold with such primitive dread? Perhaps not; nevertheless, we have borrowed that phrase from the past and use it today to describe a quite different hour of the wolf: that wakeful time in the middle of the night when fear of failure, or pain from a remembered humiliation, or grief over a lost love haunts the forest of the human heart.

In January 1925, when diphtheria struck Nome, Alaska, the only way to supply the city's doctor with serum to treat the epidemic was by using relay teams of dog-sled drivers. Seventeen teams of Eskimo, Indian, and white drivers took one hundred and seventy hours to traverse the thousand miles to Nome over an old freight-delivery route known as the Iditarod Trail.

In March 1973 the first commemorative Iditarod Trail Race was run over the same route taken by those gallant teams of men and dogs a half-century earlier. Today the Iditarod Trail runs officially from Anchorage to Nome and is described as being one thousand and forty-nine miles in length—one thousand miles in memory of that first race, with forty-nine miles added to honor Alaska's place as the forty-ninth state of the union. In truth, as it follows a course that varies every year, the annual Iditarod Trail Race is closer to thirteen hundred miles long.

The names and descriptions of racers in the following story are fictitious; the descriptions of fierce Alaska storms, treacherous mountain slopes, and profound stress endured each year by eager drivers and their dogs are not.

# 1

JAKE STEPPED OUT OF THE TENT and shivered in the cold January air. He peered at the thermometer tied to the tent pole: five below zero. He turned to study the moving branches of the spruce tree behind him. The wind was light, about six miles an hour out of the northwest. Good; it was the kind of weather the dogs liked best. He zipped his down-filled parka and snapped frost out of the cuffs of his insulated mittens.

Ordinary observations, ordinary acts. Except that nothing was ordinary anymore; maybe it never would be again. After all, the Snow Walker had come for Danny Yumiat ten days ago. *The Snow Walker* . . . Jake shivered again. Was he still kidding himself, or would disguising the truth with an old Alaskan image like that really make things easier?

Jake hunched his shoulders against the morning chill and squinted across the snow-covered valley toward the Talkeetna Mountains. He half-expected to see etched there some evidence of his loss. There was none. The world continued to turn relentlessly on its axis; the sky was as pearly and indifferent as it'd been a week and a half ago.

Well, at least a skiff of snow had fallen during the night. Along with the cool temperature, a dusting of powder snow,

1

light as talcum on the hard-packed trail, would pep the dogs up, would make the remainder of the journey seem more of a lark than a dreary condolence visit.

Each of the eleven huskies, with the exception of Skosha, who'd slept in the tent with him, was still curled asleep in the shallow snow hole Jake had scooped for it the night before and lined with spruce boughs. The dogs' thick, plumey tails, called brushes when one spoke of the husky breed, were folded neatly across their muzzles in order to warm the cold air before it was breathed in. Was that a strategy, Jake wondered idly, remembered from distant days when dogs had freely roamed the tundra and been brothers to the wolves?

By degrees the sky overhead blushed peach, rose, paled at last to mauve. In a few moments, Jake realized, dawn would be pulled from her hideaway behind the Talkeetnas and flung across the valley where he stood. Then the taiga —months ago Danny explained that the Russian word meant land of little sticks, or an area covered by a growth of stunted spruce and young birch saplings—would be filled with silver sentinels. Next the snowfields on the mountain slopes would become a polished wasteland, populated only by Arctic foxes and snowshoe rabbits. It was a familiar scene; since race training started in September, Jake had run the trail with Danny more times than he could count. Now, of course, it all seemed different.

"It *is* different," Jake reminded himself out loud. The words hung on the chilly morning air, three round, frosty puffs, only inches from his nose. This time he was traveling to Nyotek alone. This time Danny Yumiat was dead.

# 2

JAKE pushed his long yellow hair impatiently out of his eyes and knelt to pry an aluminum tent peg out of the snow. Dead. That word was everything Danny Yumiat himself had never been: closed, contained, silent. He'd been mistaken, Jake decided; to call death the Snow Walker didn't help after all. Dead was still dead.

Just the same, it wasn't fair. Ten days ago Danny'd been so alive! He'd smiled widely and often, his square white teeth gleaming out of his dark face as from some slick TV ad for toothpaste. But even more remarkable than his appearance was the fact that Danny always seemed to know exactly who he was, what he wanted, where he wanted to go.

"Not like me, that's for sure," Jake mused.

At the sound of his voice, Skosha trotted to his side, nudged him with her shoulder, probed affectionately at his cheek with a cold, damp nose. Jake turned, grateful, and aimed a kiss at the furred depression between the husky's eyes.

"Geez, Mathiessen," he groaned, glad no one was around to see what he'd just done, "you're a dim bulb! Cowboys plant smackers on their ponies, so you lay one on your faithful pooch!" But even Skosha's amiable flirting was not enough to make him stop thinking about Danny.

One thing for sure: being an Athabascan Indian boy from a tiny village along the banks of the Tanana River hadn't cramped Danny's style. He'd just galloped through life, and everything fell into place for him: he'd been elected vice-president of his graduating class, had been nominated to the student council, was sure to have got that scholarship he'd applied for at the University of Alaska in Fairbanks.

Once Doc Smalley had allowed that Danny had "a well-rounded personality." The description made Danny sound not only whole but wholesome. Guys liked Danny; on the other hand, so did girls. *Girls.* Aliens from another galaxy, Jake thought. But Danny . . . well, Danny was a lot like Bo, back home in Minnesota. Guys like that just had it made in the shade.

Of course, when Danny came to harness his team in the dog-lot behind Smalley's Animal Clinic every afternoon after school, Jake took care to stay out of his way. He didn't have time to hang around and gawk anyway; Doc Smalley usually had at least a dozen dogs boarding, which meant a dozen dog-runs to be cleaned every day, a dozen dogs to be fed and watered.

Jake figured Danny probably paid as little attention to him, even if they each felt obliged to give the other a passing nod in recognition of the fact that they shared the same shop class three days a week. Just the same, Jake wished he'd been ready with a smart answer on the afternoon Danny'd hollered at him across the yard.

"Hey, Outsider! You ever thought about being a dog handler?" Then he grinned slyly and watched Jake scoop dog droppings into a plastic trash barrel. "I mean, a real one?"

Jake flushed. *Outsider* . . . at the beginning of his exile, he'd hated that word. As if I needed to be reminded, he thought bitterly. It bothered him less, though, after Win Smalley explained it was a label hung around the neck of any newcomer, that it only meant someone who was not lucky enough to be an Insider, someone born "in the country," as old-timers called it, or who'd at least lived in Alaska for a long time. Win qualified as an Insider now; he'd been in the country for nearly twenty years.

"Dog handler?" Jake remembered echoing foolishly. The first issue of *The Eagle,* the school paper, had carried a picture on its front page of Danny running a bunch of dogs in front of a weird-looking training cart made out of the chassis of an old Volkswagen. "Snow Isn't Here Yet, but Yumiat Trains for *The Last Great Race!*" screamed the caption. And a handler was . . . ?

By then Jake had been in the country long enough himself to know that the Last Great Race meant only one race, the thousand-mile-long Iditarod Trail Race, which began each March at Mulcahy Park in Anchorage and was held to commemorate a famous run made by dog teams in 1925 to deliver life-saving serum to children in Nome during a diphtheria epidemic. He'd had to ask Win Smalley exactly how the name was pronounced, though.

"You mean the Big I?" Doc had boomed, clapping Jake on the back with a hand as big as a stove lid. His hair was red, and even his voice seemed flame-colored. He'd worked as a steward on several of the races. "Just like it looks, Jake—Eye-dit-a-rod, that's how. It's the English version of an old Indian word, *haiditarod,* which means a distant place—and that's a pretty fair description of the village of Iditarod, all right. On Christmas Day in, oh, I think it was about 1908, a couple of prospectors hit it rich up there. Their vein didn't run very deep, though, and petered out.

Afterward Iditarod got to be well known mostly as a freight post for points even deeper in the interior of Alaska. When the serum run started, the stuff was carried to the end of the rail line, wrapped in fur so's it wouldn't freeze, then hauled by relay dog teams all the way to Nome."

Win Smalley clamped a linebacker's arm around Jake's shoulder and winked. "It's one of those yarns that warms a man's blood, right? Which is the main reason I decided to let that Yumiat kid have some space behind the clinic to use as a dog-lot while he trains for the next race. In a world gone bonkers busting things up or tearing 'em down, I figure celebrating an event like the serum run ought to give folks something else to talk about."

Big deal, Jake thought sourly. Win sounded like a representative of the Chamber of Commerce. So Yumiat was a sled-dog racing nut. Judging from most of Doc's clients, so was practically everybody else in Alaska. Even Doc had a pair of huskies, Skosha and Benjie, to haul a child's sled around the yard for Nora and baby Angus.

None of which explained what a handler was, of course. Jake hesitated before he asked. Was a handler some guy who shuffled the dogs from point A to point B, like hairy pawns on a giant chessboard? Or maybe handling was more like dandling, and you put the pooch on the point of your knee, like an uncle with a favorite nephew, and jiggled the mutt until he arfed for mercy?

"Ain't nothing mysterious about being a handler," Danny answered easily. "It's kinda like being a team manager; no big deal." He smiled a blazing, tooth-filled smile. "It's just that when a guy's got twelve or fourteen huskies to hook up before a race, it can get mighty tough if he's trying to do everything himself. You know, make sure all the dogs get in harness by chute time, see that the gangline stays straight, keep the dogs from chewing on their gear— details like that. Last year my sister helped me out. She was sharp, too, but she's in school in Seattle now, so I hafta hustle up another warm body."

Jake shrugged. "Forget it, fella," he mumbled. Dogs, even Doc's boarders, only brought Mozart to mind. Four years ago Dad had wanted to get a German shepherd and Mibsie had her heart set on an Irish setter, but when the time came to actually buy a pet, everyone agreed on a poodle because it was the only breed Mother could find that came in a color specifically called apricot.

"He's got to match the new carpet and draperies," she'd pointed out with the sort of smile that discouraged further discussion on the subject. She smoothed her already smooth hair, which was, now that Jake thought about it, suspiciously apricot-colored.

"The decorator said a coordinated look was important," she went on to explain, "and if we get a brown dog—worse yet, a red one!—why, he just wouldn't fit in." The gaucheness of getting a pet that didn't coordinate kept everyone silent. When a family set out to pick a dog, Jake thought ruefully, they could choose one that fit. When a son came along, they were obliged to take what they got.

Jake turned when he heard Danny's team careen out of the dog-lot and take off toward the mountains behind Smalley's Animal Clinic. Danny's huge, gray lead dog strained into its nylon harness, its ears flattened against its head as sleek as the ears of a wet seal. The other dogs, mouths agape and tongues lolling, labored to keep pace. Mozart's image vanished from Jake's mind, and when he met Danny in shop class again, he had an answer ready to the invitation to become a handler.

"Hey, Yumiat, what you said the other day—about helping you out and all that. I suppose I could give it a try." Besides, wasn't this one of the things Dad was on his back about almost every week on the phone? Regular calls were an agreement they'd made before he left home. "Make some new friends, Jake," Dad advised every seven days. Why, exactly, did he think it'd be so much easier in Alaska than it'd been in Minnesota?

Still, there was something Jake had to know. "But why *me*, Yumiat?" he asked. Danny was taller than he was, and Jake found himself looking up at the other boy. "You hardly know me, only seen me here in shop or out there scooping poop at Smalley's. There's got to be at least a dozen guys in this school who'd be a heckuva lot more . . ."

Danny narrowed his black eyes and smiled. "I've been watching you, Outsider," he said knowingly, as if they already shared some private understanding. What it might be was a mystery to Jake. "You're okay with Doc's dogs, see. Doc said so himself, and I figured you'd handle mine okay, too."

Jake hiked one shoulder with an indifference he did not really feel. Well, sure, it was nice to hear that a guy like Win Smalley'd given him a couple of points, but it didn't exactly take brains or talent to feed and clean up after a bunch of mutts. It wasn't like tennis or golf or racquetball, those things Dad was so expert at. "Besides, you take things slow and easy, Outsider," Danny added. "That's good in a handler. Helps keep a racing team calm, y'know."

Slow was all of a sudden a virtue? Boy, it'd be news to Dad. "Get a move on, Jake!" was a familiar order whenever the family got ready to take the boat down to Lake of the Isles or pack the car for vacation.

Danny gestured disgustedly in the direction of the class

they'd just left. "You know some of the guys in shop, Out-sider. Those turkeys don't have the right brand of pa-tience. No way would I ever ask one of 'em to be my handler!"

Shop class, of course, was something else that ticked Dad off. "*Shop?*" he'd groaned into the phone when Jake called to report on his class schedule. "You don't need shop, son. That's the kind of class a boy takes when he's not headed for the sort of career you are. *You* won't ever have to earn a living with your hands, Jake." That, of course, would not fit the Mathiessen family image. "It would be tacky, dear boy, *so* tacky," Jake could hear Mibs sniff. Who'd she think she was, anyway? Royalty?

Then Dad's voice dropped an octave, and Jake knew the treatment he was in for. Even over the phone, he could see Dad's agate-colored eyes take on a look of hawkish intent. It was a glance guaranteed to mold the response of a jury and was one of the minor reasons Dad was called the best defense lawyer in the Midwest.

"You'll be joining the firm someday, Jake, just like I joined it with my father," Dad reminded him. Then it'd be Mathiessen, Blumenthal, Brown and Mathiessen, At-torneys-at-Law, just like it used to be. "So take my advice, Jake. Sign up for stuff like Econ. Government. History, even. Why, a little history couldn't hurt you. But shop! Well, son, shop couldn't matter less." *Only to me*, Jake thought, and signed up for it anyway. For the rest of the day he'd felt independent. It was a rare feeling that never lasted long enough.

Danny, naturally, had other things on his mind; *he* needed a handler, not a law partner. "When I came down from the village three years ago—see, I have to come into town each fall to board," he explained, "on account of we

9

don't have many high schools out there in the bush—well, let me tell you, I felt like some poor pup that'd been stuck in a dog bag and shipped off to Mars!" He grinned and studied Jake with shrewd black eyes.

"There's only about twenty-three people in my whole village, y'know," he went on, "and we're all like family to each other. I felt lost, like an orphan, being out of the village like that. So the other day when ol' McNemee called your name in shop and you acted like you couldn't remember what it was, I figured I knew exactly how you felt."

"Well, you didn't," Jake was tempted to say. He hadn't wanted to remember anything, not who he was, where he came from, or why he'd been exiled for two years to a place he'd never wanted to visit for even two weeks.

"Me, I'm gonna be a lawyer for my people," Danny confided the next afternoon after they hooked up and ran the team past Win's hospital toward the Chugach Mountains.

Swell, Jake thought. I came up here to get away from lawyers, and what happens? He slouched deeper into the sled basket; on these training runs, one of his jobs would be to act as ballast. Maybe I ought to take this kid home for a visit, he mused silently. On Father's Day, no less. "Here, Dad," he'd quip, "a token of my affection. The upwardly mobile kind of kid the family ordered but didn't get. Better yet, this one even *wants* to be a lawyer."

Danny jumped the sled around a corner as Jake automatically leaned his weight into it. "Oh, sure, sometimes I wonder if I got the juice it'll take to do all the things I want to do, get through law school and all that," Danny admitted with his next breath. Jake glanced over his shoulder and was surprised to see that Danny's million-watt smile had dimmed faintly. "I mean, I'm just an Athabascan kid from a village you can't even find on the map. Then I tell myself, 'Heck, Yumiat, give it your best shot!' That's all anybody can do, right?" The next smile was another wide million-watter.

Jake envied the ease with which Danny dismissed his doubts. For some people it wasn't that easy. Not only was I never a credit to my family, Jake thought as they flew down the snowy trail in a fog of ice crystals raised by the dogs' racing feet, all I ever wanted was out. *Out.* Why else would a person pull a stop-the-world-I-want-to-get-off routine on his own parents and sister, people he was supposed to love and who were supposed to love him back? Well, what happened after *that* little caper, Jake reflected, was that the whole family freaked out and could only repeat the two words that were now stitched onto his heart like varsity letters onto a letterman's sweater: *Take Jake!* Take him, somebody, anybody, and don't bring him back until he's a Boy We Can All Be Proud Of.

Jake frowned, pulled up the hood of his parka, cinched its drawstring. All that was ancient history. Skosha pressed her nose into his cupped palm. Jake reached for her ear and fondled it absentmindedly. He looked down at her. The muzzle of a Siberian husky was a lot like that of a fox, he decided, neat and narrow, and in repose such dogs' lips seemed to curl into a soft, knowing smile. Once, at the supper table, baby Angus had grinned and Doc Smalley had marveled, "Now isn't that sweet as the smile of a husky pup!"

Skosha was Doc's dog, of course, but there were moments, like this one, when Jake was sure Skosha loved *him.* Love. Geez. It was just another four-letter word. Weird—

11

now that he was living three thousand miles from Minnesota with a family named Smalley whose existence hadn't mattered until a year ago, it was hard to remember what'd been so wrong with his old life that he'd tried to . . .

Jake clamped his jaw tight. The memory of those old, dark moments still had the power to make him feel small and lost and foolish. No matter what'd happened to Danny ten days ago, it was still easier to ponder the other boy's fate than examine his own too closely.

While Skosha watched attentively, Jake collapsed the blue nylon tent he'd pitched open-ended near the base of a scrawny spruce the night before. In front of the opening, a safe distance from the overhanging tree limbs, he'd built a small fire of twigs and debris salvaged from under the snow that covered the valley floor. The three closed sides of the tent collected the heat like a baffle, and with Skosha by his side he'd slept through the cold Alaska night as snug as if he'd been home in his old bed in Minneapolis.

Jake loosened another tent peg. That bed, a handsome pine four-poster as big as a boat, transported all the way from Denmark by his great-grandfather in 1873, belonged to some jerk named Jacob Arthur Mathiessen, didn't it? He was a wimpy, lonely, not-too-tall character with pale hair and flat feet whose initials, unfortunately, spelled Jam. He'd gotten that nickname back in third grade from some smart aleck whose own had long since been forgotten. "Good ol' Jam/ Always in a jam!" That schoolyard jingle had haunted Jake from the moment it'd been invented. Worse, it'd turned out to be true.

Jake gathered up all the tent pegs, then rested his elbows on his bent knees. He glanced toward the brilliant white slopes of the Talkeetnas. Wasn't time supposed to go only one way—forward? So how come I'm remembering a name like Jam, Jake wondered, or my old bed, a dog named Mozart, a living room painted apricot? I'm being pulled back, back. I'm not free yet, might never be. Which doesn't make any sense at all, he thought, because I've been gone from home a year and right now I'm on my way to a village called Nyotek to take nine dogs from this eleven-dog team back to Danny's family, and the kid everybody used to call Jam is dead now, too. Just as dead as a boy named Danny Yumiat will ever be.

# 3

∴

J AKE STACKED ALL THE TENT PEGS on top
of the folded tent, then rolled it, tied it, and tossed
it into the forward part of the sled basket with his
nylon sleeping bag. All the heavier gear—a two-burner
Coleman stove for emergencies, a fifty-pound sack of dry
meal for the dogs, frozen plastic packages of stew for himself—had already been stashed near the driving bow.

"Keep the center of gravity low and toward the back of
the sled when you load it," Danny had advised on their
first trip to Nyotek. "That way the sled rides nose up and
you won't have to worry so much about busting up your
brush bow."

The brush bow, a piece of curved wood on the nose of
the sled, Danny explained, was to a dog sled what a
bumper was to a car—it deflected damage to the body of
the sled, its cargo, and the driver—but not if the driver tore
it off in a brush pile on a narrow trail or snagged it on a
low-hanging tree limb when the sled warped a corner too
close.

Danny had handled the sled, the dogs, the dangers of the
trail just like he handled his life, Jake thought enviously.
Danny's life trained him for such expertise, he mused on,
just like mine was supposed to train me to want to be a
credit to the Mathiessen family name.

14

"I've been hanging onto a driving bow since I was six or seven years old," Danny once boasted cheerfully. " 'Course, a kid that age, and I was a skinny squirt to boot, only has enough strength to wrestle one or two dogs along a trail. But I worked my way up to a three-dog team by the time I was nine, then five dogs, running all the time with a single leader. By the time I was fifteen, I had a twelve-dog team and two good leaders and I'd won a few races around Nyotek. I knew for sure I'd try my luck at the Iditarod someday. Wow, the Last Great Race! Has the ring of destiny about it, right? I used to trace on a map the names of all the villages a guy's gotta pass through on his way to Nome, and I'd go to sleep at night wondering what it'd be like. . . ."

Jake stirred the ashes of last night's fire, added fresh wood, and set a can of clean snow to melt in the coals to make drinking water for the dogs and a cup of breakfast cocoa for himself. He added the snow by handfuls, making sure it melted thoroughly before he added more; otherwise the snow would scorch on the hot metal and have an unpleasant, metallic taste. It was one more wrinkle he'd learned from Danny. When the water finally was steaming, Jake added it to some dry dog pellets, poured several tablespoons of fish oil over the mixture, and gave each team member a portion on a tin pie plate.

The Last Great Race . . . yes, those three words had the ring of destiny in them, all right, but what else could you call a dogsled race that took at least two weeks to run, traversed a thousand miles of muskeg, tundra, river ice, and mountains that sloped at forty degrees? Racers would be tormented by winds of up to sixty miles an hour and temperatures of forty degrees below zero, Doc had said. Dogs would go lame or get diarrhea and have to be dropped from the race; drivers would suffer frostbite, dehydration, and hallucinations brought on by fatigue and physical hardship.

"And I wasn't even crazy about Boy Scout camp-outs," Jake muttered to himself. Anybody who wanted to run the Iditarod had to have a lot of self-confidence or be an Insider. "Let's face it, Danny made it on both counts," he admitted to Skosha, who'd finished her breakfast and returned to sit beside him. "That's why I still don't understand why he . . ."

Jake firmed his jaw, spooned cocoa and dry milk powder into a metal mug, and poured hot water over the mixture. Cut the crappola, Mathiessen, he advised himself. Some deeds can't be undone, and some questions don't have answers; didn't you learn all about that in Minneapolis? He stirred his cocoa, drank it hastily, and scalded his throat.

"C'mon, Skosha!" he snapped, much more sharply than he'd meant to. He was angry with himself, with Danny. None of it was her fault. The husky flattened her ears apologetically, and Jake buried his fingers in the midnight-colored fur of her neck ruff. It was as deep and silky as a prime fox pelt. "Hey, babe," he whispered, contrite, "you're a good girl, hear? A good girl . . ."

She was, too. Until Danny died, Skosha had never run in the lead. Actually, she and Benjie only ran in the team because Danny was short two dogs; he'd intended to get replacements in a few weeks. But right from the start, Skosha seemed to understand what leading was all about: she made sure the other dogs didn't slack-line by setting a pace that kept the line tight. As for letting her sleep in the tent last night—Jake grinned sheepishly down at her—that had been more for his sake than for hers. The truth was, it'd been a little scary to find himself alone on the trail.

16

When he'd been with Danny, he'd never noticed how much the empty white space impinged from every direction.

Knowing it was hook-up time, Skosha bounded eagerly toward the sled, a slim-legged, black-and-silver husky who wore a harlequin's black mask across her face, out of which two cornflower-blue eyes glowed like a pair of Arctic stars. Such eyes, Danny said, pale rather than dark, would be called "watch eyes" in any other dog breed, but in a husky they were as common as blue eyes on a human and marked their possessor as having descended from a long line of Siberian ancestors.

Skosha had made other trips to Nyotek and knew they were on the last leg of their journey. She fairly vibrated under Jake's fingers as he slipped a padded Fishback harness made out of nylon webbing over her head, then drew her right front leg through its leg hole, next the left, and tugged the harness snugly down over her spine before snapping her to the gangline.

"Your turn, Sundance!" Jake called. "Be sure to call the dogs by their names," Danny had told him when he was learning to be a handler. "Don't just holler, 'Hey, you!' Out on the trail each dog's gotta recognize his own name and pay attention whenever he hears it."

Jake unhooked Sundance from his stake chain under the spruce tree, and the big cinnamon-colored dog hustled with misleading eagerness to his place in the left wheel position. That term, borrowed from mule freighters, meant the position directly in front of the sled basket. If the lead dog supplied the brains of the team, Danny had explained, laughing, then the wheel dogs were its brawn; they supplied the first hard pull to get the sled started, had the toughest work pulling uphill, with the full weight of the load directly behind them. Sundance and Roger, both large dogs with traces of malamute in their backgrounds, were naturals for the wheel spot.

Jake knew from past experience, though, that Sundance's early morning displays of energy could be short-lived. "All sass and flash, aren't you, fella?" Jake chided. In another hour Sundance might need to hear the sound of the jingler in his ear, a noisemaker Danny'd fashioned out of bottlecaps strung on a piece of wire and held as a gypsy would hold a tambourine. Sundance has a lot in common with my old Minnesota pal, Bo, Jake thought; Bo had been flashy and lazy, too. Jake snapped Sundance to the gangline, which Skosha kept pulled tight as a fiddle string. Dad said Bo was a real basket case, that he'd never amount to anything, no matter who his old man was. Or was Bo the one he was talking about? Maybe it was me he really meant, Jake thought. Jake shoved that suspicion from his mind and tapped Sundance lightly on the fanny.

"Bet you'd shape up in a hurry if Tanana was here," he teased.

Tanana wasn't, though. He'd been Danny's command leader, a part-wolf dog who'd been trained to respond to verbal orders. Skosha was just beginning to understand what the words "Gee!" and "Haw!" really meant. Sundance, as if he realized he'd just been compared to his old teammate and found lacking, hung his head in shame.

Next Jake hooked up the six team dogs, Benjie, Rab, Cookie, Paddy, Juno, and Heidi, who ran in front of the wheel dogs. "Now you, Popcorn, and you, too, Alex." Popcorn and Alex pulled in the swing position, directly behind the leader; it was their job to make sure the rest of the dogs stayed on the trail, especially around turns, and didn't head off into deep snow.

Popcorn, a crossbred from a dog-lot up at Stony River, had a tufted, butter-colored coat that indicated some terrier heritage. He really does look as if he's made out of popcorn, Jake thought, glued together with sugar syrup and propped up on four long, pipe cleaner legs. Alex was short for Alexyov; Danny claimed the dog's forebears came from the famous Kolyma River Valley, across the Chukchi Sea, where the first Siberian sled dogs had been bred. *Danny claimed . . . Danny said . . .* Danny, Danny, Danny!

He knew it was pointless, but Jake let his thoughts drift back again to the accident. Not even Red Pulaski, who'd twice run in the Iditarod himself and now owned Arctic Outfitters, had been able to understand exactly what'd gone wrong. Oh, the how of it was plain to everyone: Danny and his part-wolf lead dog, Tanana, had drowned. It was the why of it that still nagged at Jake.

"Geez, Yumiat," he accused, as if by some miracle Danny were back at his elbow, that familiar blazing smile pasted on his wide, brown face, "you had too many smarts to cross that river where you did, even on a practice run." Besides, Jake wondered uneasily, why couldn't you have waited for me that afternoon? Instead, Danny had skipped shop, said he wanted to give the dogs a long session, claimed he didn't want to hang around until Jake finished chores at Doc's.

But maybe Danny shouldn't have been running the team at all, what with everything else that'd been on his mind. Three days earlier he'd screwed up on an important Soc Sci test, and the scholarship exam that was coming up had him acting as anxious as Jake sometimes felt after a chewing-out by Dad. Not that Danny ever let on much about how he felt about stuff like that; mostly, he just covered it all up with another one of his famous smiles.

19

And since it was January, *venen nuyilqu'i*, or the-month-getting-light-again, as Danny's people called it, it wasn't as if Danny couldn't see where he was going. Nobody knew better than he did that a person shouldn't try to cross the Knik River, no matter how stable the ice looked. It was Danny, after all, who'd talked about how changes in the jet stream that flowed along the Gulf of Alaska kept the Knik from freezing solid as it had in bygone days, had warned an amateur like Jake away from it.

Since the ice didn't freeze solid to the river bottom as it did on inland rivers, the weight of the ice sometimes caused it to sink. Then river water oozed up over the ice and refroze there in layers slick as glass. Red Pulaski said that a century before German explorers called it *Aufeis*, or ice on ice. To make matters even worse, the weak ice was corroded from below by swiftly running river water and eventually became rotten in spots, like decay on a bad tooth. Sometimes gaps in the ice, called overflow holes, opened on its surface.

I wonder how long it took Danny to realize after he hit the *Aufeis* that he couldn't save himself? Jake asked himself for the hundredth time. The slick ice around the overflow hole would've resisted traction from sled runner or boot. Had Danny grabbed his snow hook, tried to beat it into the ice to hold himself and the team away from the gaping hole? Had he known that, once sucked into the water, he'd be as helpless as a bit of flotsam going down a bathtub drain?

On Saturday, two days after the accident, when the mushers who congregated every afternoon at the Arctic Outfitters decided to go out to look at the overflow hole, Jake let himself be carried along, too. He had to go, he told himself. Danny's surviving dogs had wandered into the tiny village of Knik, dragging their broken sled behind them, and someone would eventually have to take them home to Nyotek. He might as well be that someone.

But once at Knik Jake found himself hanging back, trailing behind Red Pulaski and the others, wondering why he hadn't let them take care of Danny's dogs. He shivered; even in the hard light of midday, the overflow hole was ominous to behold. He tried to look away.

He imagined Danny slipping, clawing at the mirrorlike surface of the ice. Had an orange Arctic sun been reflected there, he wondered idly, cold and indifferent on Danny's final afternoon? Then Jake saw Danny let go of the driving bow and slide forward on his knees to cut the gangline, watched as Danny got tangled in Tanana's lines when he tried to cut the wolf-dog loose. Horror rose in Jake as he saw Danny and Tanana spin like windblown leaves across the sloping *Aufeis* toward the black water. . . . It plucked greedily at them. . . . A moment later their faces were pale and pleading under the ice and it was too late, too late.

Red Pulaski had halted and turned to wait for Jake to catch up. "Sure ain't a pretty sight," he'd agreed, as if he were a mind reader. Jake shivered again, and it was not the January wind that chilled him to the bone. "Heck, Danny knew as well as the rest of us that the Knik don't freeze like it used to," Red had grumbled on. He'd reached out to massage Jake's shoulder with a sympathetic hand. "Thing is, nobody deserves a fate like that, especially a kid like Danny." Jake was too numb to answer. Besides, it'd take too long to explain certain things to Red, not that he'd probably want to listen anyway.

To begin with, was there any way to make a man like Red understand that the interior of the emergency room at the County Medical Center back home looked as smooth and white as the *Aufeis?* The overflow hole, after all, was not the first time Jake had stood close enough to death to touch it. The first time had been so weird, though: in spite of the fact that his injury a year ago had been severe, Jake remembered that he'd felt no real pain, only a spreading warmth deep inside his neck, right under his ear.

"Can you hear me, kid?" the intern wanted to know. Jake had been able to see him clearly; he looked far too young to be a real doctor, and his mustache was a frail wisp above his white coat. Jake had nodded yes. "Start at ninety-nine and count backward," he'd been told after being warned that the needle in his arm might sting.

The needle in my arm might sting? Jake remembered he'd felt like laughing then. Hey, he wanted to explain, don't you realize I just tried to kill myself?

Instead, he started to count. "Ninety-nine, ninety-eight, ninety-seven. . . ." He could feel a bubble in his throat. Blood? The edges of the emergency room darkened, turned inward like the petals of an evil flower. "This kid almost bought the farm tonight," Dr. Droopy Mustache called to someone nearby. Maybe he was talking to Dad; Mom and Mibs had probably been called, too. The light overhead turned into a spinning disk, a leftover piece of wizardry from *Star Wars.* Jake remembered he'd gotten all the way to ninety-three before everything became compressed and black. Death was exactly like he'd hoped it'd be. He held his arms wide, grabbed onto it, hugged it close.

Only he didn't die like he was supposed to. The bullet from Great-Grandfather's pistol had somehow threaded its way neatly downward between his esophagus and spinal column and lodged itself in the fleshy part of his shoulder. Just one more darned thing he couldn't do right the first time! He'd healed quick on the outside, though; the doctor said the wound was clean and would leave only a small scar. But the inside of his head was as messed up as ever, filled with riddles that didn't have answers. Like, how did a guy ever find out who he was if his father was a legend? Like, was it possible to make friends with somebody who looked like a silver hawk?

Jake licked his lips and shrugged off Red's sympathetic hand. The harsh wind off the Chugach Mountains froze the saliva on Jake's lips; later, he knew, his mouth would blister and peel. He backed slowly away from the overflow hole; he'd already seen more than he needed to see. More than that, it was unnerving to realize he was standing on the very spot where Danny'd died, yet was still possessed by his own past. Dummy, he thought angrily, don't you know you can't run far enough or fast enough to ever catch hold of what you're looking for?

You can't run far enough or fast enough. . . .

Jake studied the back of Red Pulaski's orange parka and licked his lips again. The idea bloomed over him with unexpected, lunatic clarity. It was stupid, of course. He should forget it. He wasn't experienced enough, not to mention brave enough to do it. The Last Great Race . . . Danny said it had the ring of destiny about it, that he'd traced on a map the names of all the villages a guy had to pass through on his thousand-mile journey to Nome. But Danny was dead now; he'd never be able to run the race himself. Somebody else will have to do it for him, Jake thought. What if that someone turned out to be me?

# 4

## ∴

JAKE LEANED ACROSS THE DRIVING BOW
and made sure his load was securely lashed down.
The sled, a loaner from Red Pulaski, was made out
of molded aluminum tubing. "Metal won't ever know
snow like wood does," had been Danny's firm opinion.
"Metal can't warp around corners like wood; just ain't
flexible enough. Someday I'm gonna have me a dandy
sled made out of birch, Jake. It'll be ten times better'n
this old beat-up thing!" He'd smiled then and thumped
the bow of his training sled with disgust, a sled that now
lay in pieces in the woods near the village of Knik.

Jake snapped the snow hook out of a snow bank; the
three-pronged metal claw, fastened to a snub rope that was
tied to the sled bridle, had held the sled in place while he'd
harnessed the team. He released the brake with his right
foot. "H*iiiiii*ke!" he hollered to the dogs, and pedaled
hard with his left foot to help them break the runners free
from the frozen snow crust.

Skosha jumped out before he'd completely given the
command, stretching the gangline tauter than before, and
the other dogs leaned eagerly into their harnesses. When
the whole team was moving easily, Jake stopped pedaling
and settled both feet firmly on the polyethylene foot-

grippers that covered the top side of the sled runners. The dogs' movement raised a fog of fresh powder snow, and Jake peered through it to appraise the sky overhead. It was nearly ten A.M., he judged; he'd be in Nyotek by late afternoon.

Even if there'd been a telephone in the village, he'd still have made a personal visit to ask Danny's parents for the use of Danny's team. It was not the sort of request a person could make any other way. The one thing he didn't want to do was chase around Anchorage trying to hustle up some mutts that had racing experience. It was true that dogs were loaned back and forth between racers. The problem was, *he* was still labeled an Outsider. People would look at him as if he were crazy if he told them he wanted to run the Big I.

If he'd just wanted to go out and buy dogs, of course Dad would've sent him some extra money. Two days before, over the phone, Jake had broached the subject, without telling Dad exactly what he planned to do. "You need dogs, Jam? Just tell me how many and what kind," had been Dad's reply.

"They gotta be trained dogs, Dad," Jake answered. "This is a tough sport. Most guys've been working their teams at least since September. Actually, I guess I'll make a trip up to Danny's village and ask if . . . "

"Village? What village? Danny who?" He wants me to have a friend, Jake thought, but he's afraid anybody I pick will turn out to be like Bo.

"Danny Yumiat, Dad." Right after the accident he'd written to all of them—Mother and Mibsie, too—to tell them what'd happened to Danny. Didn't they even read their mail? "Remember, Dad, I told you about Danny. We were in gym class together, among other things." The class

25

SOUTH HIGH COMMUNITY LIBRARY

was shop, but there was no point in getting into all that again. "Danny died, remember? Two weeks ago."

"Oh. Died. Yes, I think I remember something . . . you said in your letter he was hit by a . . . "

Even in letters Dad couldn't pay attention. "Danny went through the ice on the Knik River, Dad. He drowned." It was an accident, Jake thought of adding. Danny was not the kind of kid to check out the way your loving son tried to.

Jake didn't bother explaining it wasn't his own idea to go to Nyotek. "If you want to ease into the dog-racing scene, kid, why don't you borrow Danny's team?" Red Pulaski had suggested. "You can't buy those dogs. Danny's folks, much less that sister of his, would never in the world sell them to you. But picking up some loaners for a season ain't uncommon at all. You were Danny's friend; it might please 'em a whole lot to loan the team to you until spring comes around."

"Danny's folks'd loan me dogs?" Jake echoed. No matter how often he'd gone to the village with Danny, he had the feeling he'd never gotten to know the Yumiats very well. Danny's father was slender and smiled a lot; his English was a little fractured, and he told jokes Jake didn't understand. Danny's mother wore her gray hair in a long plait down her back and was so quiet that a person hardly knew she was around. As for Danny's sister, well, she was still in Seattle and had never been in the village any of the times Jake visited there.

"Danny's sister has got Tanana's littermate, y'know," Red pointed out. He pulled thoughtfully at his beard. "I've been told by folks who oughta know that her dog is as good a leader as Tanana ever was. Now whether you could borrow *that* dog from the Yumiats is another matter.

But as it is, Jake, you only got that little Skosha. She ain't a Park Avenue poodle, truth to tell, but she ain't the kind of dog that'll win you any sprint races, either."

Red would never suspect I have anything but a sprint race in mind, Jake realized. It was Danny, after all, who had the sort of experience it took to claim the dream of running the Iditarod, a dream that now floated under the icy waters of the Gulf of Alaska.

But perhaps Red Pulaski was the bush philosopher he fancied himself to be, Jake decided later, for he'd added softly as he peered through the steamed-over windows of Arctic Outfitters, "Well, dreams die hard, don't they, sonny? Even if they were only the kind you shared with someone else."

At noon Jake stopped to check the dogs' footpads for ice. Each dog flopped happily on its side in the thin winter sunshine and let Jake groom each paw carefully with his bare fingers, plucking out the offending ice balls. A full-blooded Siberian like Skosha tended to have paws that were heavily furred between the toes, giving her feet a webbed appearance and making the collection of ice less of a problem. Popcorn, on the other hand, with his part-terrier heritage and thin coat, collected more ice on his feet than any of his teammates.

Jake made another twig fire, melted snow again in the metal bucket, and gave each dog two cupfuls of lukewarm water in its own dish. "If you give 'em cold water, they gotta warm it up to body temperature later in their bellies," Danny had said, "which uses up calories they could spend better on the trail. Way I figure, it pays to make things as easy on the dogs as I can."

Into each dish Jake dropped a small piece of salmon to

flavor the water. Chum salmon, lighter in color than the famous dark red king salmon, had a half-century earlier been dubbed "dog salmon," because it was used mainly as food for sled teams. Jake knew that he didn't really have to go to such elaborate lengths for the dogs, flavoring their drinking water and stripping spruce branches to line their beds at night, on such an easy trip as this one. Just the same, being sure the team didn't get dehydrated and that each member was warm and comfortable at night made him feel as efficient as Danny.

When the dogs had rested, and after he'd warmed some frozen stew for himself, Jake resumed his journey. The last leg of the trip took longer than he'd expected, and the sky overhead had the soft metallic look of pewter when he arrived at last on the familiar snow ridge above Nyotek.

Below, no one stirred. Had the whole village gone off, Jake wondered, to mourn Danny at some peculiar wailing ceremony of grief? He rolled his mittened fingers slowly around the driving bow of his aluminum sled. There were so many things he didn't know about Danny, about Danny's people. Suddenly Jake felt like more of a stranger in a strange land than ever before.

Nevertheless he lightly depressed the sled brake and mushed the team slowly down the white slope into the village. No dog ran out to bark a welcome as before; no chimney trailed a thin blue ribbon of fragrant smoke. Most of the village homes, about eight in number, were simple earthen dugouts. Only their wood-framed doorways protruded from the snow. Near Danny's house a crimson scarf fluttered from a willow pole planted in the snow like a walking stick, an eerie reminder of someone who'd come and gone through that door. It was the scarf Danny had always worn, Apache-style, whenever he raced.

Later Jake realized he'd been so mesmerized by that red

fabric fluttering on the winter air that he hadn't heard anyone behind him. It was a growing sense of somebody's-watching-me that made him finally turn around, and there she was.

There was no mistaking who she was, though. She looked so much like Danny, nobody would've mistaken her for anybody else's sister. She was nearly as tall as Danny had been and, in her down-filled parka and fur-trimmed caribou mukluks, seemed almost as sturdy. That was where any similarity ended, however, for her eyes were narrow and hostile, and her mouth, instead of being ready for a toothpaste commercial, was a bitter slash in her dark face. If Danny had loved life, Jake thought, his sister looked as if she could string together a few well-chosen words to describe what she thought of it.

"Let me tell you, kid, that girl knows darned near as much about mushing a team of fishburners as Danny ever did," Red Pulaski had said with a shake of his head when Jake said he hoped she wouldn't be in the village when he went to ask for loaners.

"People at school—well, one guy who knew her pretty well told me she was a little crazy," Jake had complained.

"Crazy? Naw!" Red guffawed. "Danny's sister is just partial to the Old Ways, that's all. I think it was a mistake, her being sent out of state to school. She shoulda stayed Inside, just like Danny did. Anyway, I heard some bozo got smart with her one night in a supermarket down there in Seattle. She had a *ulu* in her pocket, so the story goes, and she chased him three blocks down the street with it." Red grinned, thinking of the lively scene that had been created in far-off Seattle. "Guess I'd rather grab a loco moose by the left hind leg than tangle with Kamina Yumiat," he sighed. "At any rate, that's when some nitwit took to calling her Krazy Kate."

Jake cleared his throat nervously and tried to smile at the girl who faced him. A *ulu* was also called a woman's knife; it had a wood or ivory handle and a short, curved blade that made it ideal for scraping tallow from a caribou hide, chopping wild berries, or scaling a fish. Jake noticed that Kamina Yumiat had one fist stuffed into the pocket of her jacket and hoped fervently that her fingers were not curled around her famous *ulu*.

Belatedly, Jake realized that Kamina was by no means alone. With her free hand she held a dog on a short, braided rawhide lead. If there'd been no question that she was Danny's sister, there was even less doubt that the dog sitting quietly at her knee was Tanana's littermate. He was only a shade darker than the platinum snowfields on the Talkeetna slopes, just as Tanana had been, and his long muzzle and deep forehead hinted at the wolf blood that was supposed to run in his veins.

"Kate," Jake began, and immediately wished he could bite off his tongue and spit it out. How dumb could a guy get? "What I mean is, Kamina," he blundered on, hoping she hadn't noticed, "I . . . uh, see, a few months ago, Danny asked me to be his handler, and after the . . . the accident, I decided maybe I would try to . . ."

She didn't let him finish. She gave him a thin, hard smile that was only a grim stretching of closed lips over clenched teeth. "I know perfectly well who you are, Outsider," Kamina Yumiat told him in a voice that sounded like splitting candle ice. Danny had used that word, Outsider, with a sly, forgiving smile in his black eyes; his sister used it like a curse.

"What's even plainer," she added bitterly, "is that you also know some fools go around calling me Krazy Kate."

30

# 5

## ∶

J AKE KNEW HE WAS TURNING RED. That long line of Danish ancestors had left him with hair so pale it was almost white and skin so fair it showed every emotion, especially embarrassment. He hunkered down and began to fuss needlessly with the team. He felt grateful when the dogs pressed eagerly against his knees, each determined to claim its fair share of the unexpected attention.

"Listen, Kamina, I didn't mean for that to come out like it must've sounded to you," he tried to explain, glad for once that his hair fell like a window shade over his eyes. "It was a dumb thing to say. Besides, I know it isn't even true. I would've come out here sooner, too, except that . . ." Except how did a person find exactly the right words to tell the parents and sister of a dead buddy that it wasn't fair? Accidents happen, he'd thought of saying, but nothing this bad should ever have happened to Danny. The words sounded weak. Wimpy. Ineffectual. All the things he'd been sent to Alaska never to be again.

Jake hazarded a sneaky upward glance through his window shade. Maybe she'd had time to soften up a little. It would sure make the job of asking for some loaners a lot less awkward. But he could see that she hadn't softened at all. The face that stared down at him was as hard and impassive as those he'd seen carved in soapstone by native craftsmen and sold in tourist shops on the main streets of Anchorage.

"Is it still kind of hard for you to believe, too?" he asked simply. "Sometimes it seems like a dream to me, like tomorrow things will be just like they used to be. I think I can understand how all of you must feel. Danny was special; everybody thought so." Maybe Kamina Yumiat could accept honest words like those, Jake hoped. No, apparently not. She continued to glare down at him with the angriest black eyes he'd ever seen.

Does she think it's my fault? Jake wondered. Or maybe he'd overlooked the obvious: maybe she wasn't really as fluent in English as those first two sentences she'd spat at him led him to believe. The problem was, only two Athabascan words came to mind—*ehu,* which meant terrific, and *idahdi,* or hello, friend—neither of which seemed to exactly fit the present situation.

Or maybe she really was a little crazy, just like that turkey at school claimed. She sure looked, well, not like any female person Jake had ever known before. He thought of his sister, Mibsie, so slim and silver, and so conscious of being a girl. Girls. That was another old problem. Other than Mibs, he'd never really known any close up. Bo had lots of women. That's what he called them, too—"my women." They weren't women, of course. They were just girls, but that's what he liked to call them. Plural, naturally, and always pretty. "*You'd* get the ones who oughta be out only on Halloween, Mathiessen," he used to gloat. In all the time he'd known Bo, Jake realized, he somehow never had a smart answer for remarks like that. But one thing for sure, Bo would take a very dim view of a girl like Kamina Yumiat.

Jake squirmed inside his parka and felt entirely too warm. It was plain there was not much sense wasting time trying to convince this girl about anything. But the trip out to Nyotek was a long one, two days out of Anchorage and two days back. He was lucky his grades had been good enough that he could get a couple of days off school. That settled it, Jake decided. He stood up, squared his shoulders, and told Kamina the truth.

"Actually, I came out here to ask you a favor," he blurted. He took a deep breath. Now he could see that she was almost, but not quite, as tall as he was. It was something to be grateful for. Imagine asking a favor from a girl as forbidding as she was if you had to look up at her?

"See, I'd like to borrow Danny's dogs. Plus a couple more, if you got any good ones around. I know it sounds crazy," he went on, wishing he'd picked a different word than crazy, "but I decided to enter the Iditarod race myself. For Danny. It's kind of . . . well, kind of a memorial gesture."

Kamina Yumiat stared at him. "There's a guy in Anchorage, his name's Red Pulaski," Jake heard himself rush witlessly on, "and he said you had a dog out here who'd been whelped in the same litter as Danny's leader, and I thought maybe if I could . . ."

Jake studiously avoided looking right into her eyes and instead fixed his own on the dog Kamina held possessively at her side. The dog regarded him with an impassive golden gaze. Its forehead was broader than that of a husky and its ears were much larger and less rounded at the tips. Jake got an uncomfortable feeling that the wolf-dog understood every word he had to say.

Jake looked back at Kamina and cranked his mouth into a grin. He'd try to disarm her. Bo said you had to disarm a

33

girl if you wanted to score. Flatter her. Joke around. Be easy, relaxed. Not that I really want to score (exactly what did that mean, anyhow?), Jake thought, all I want to do is borrow a good lead dog from her and maybe a couple of extra team dogs to replace Skosha and Benjie so they can go back to being Win's pets like they used to be.

"Well, he sure looks like Tanana, doesn't he?" Jake heard himself chirp brightly. "Guess you could say they were a couple of ice cubes knocked off the same glacier, huh?" As a joke, it was pretty bad. Worse, Kamina gave no sign of being disarmed or the least bit entertained. Her expression, he decided, ought to be called Frozen Solid.

I suppose she thinks it's too bad it wasn't me who got caught out on the *Aufeis*, he mused. She doesn't know that a year ago I would've been glad to jump into that overflow hole, would've thought it was great to be food for the fish. But things are different now; now all I want to do is borrow some pooches and run a thousand miles to Nome.

"You?" Kamina finally hissed in amazement. Jake flinched as if she'd slapped him. "*You* want to enter the Iditarod? Boy, I hope somebody catches you quick and locks you up, on account of you are goofy enough to be a danger to yourself and innocent bystanders." Well, at least that proved there wasn't anything wrong with her command of the English language.

Jake felt obliged to defend himself. "I've been working with Danny since September," he explained hastily. "He let me drive the dogs lots of times. Some Saturdays he let me run 'em in small bush races, y'know, five- and ten-milers. Sometimes I came in third or fourth or fifth. Nothing great, and I know it was mostly the dogs that did it, but I thought maybe if I could lay my hands on a good lead dog. . . ." He fastened his glance significantly on the

34

dog at her side and realized he had no idea what its name was.

"Denedi," Kamina said, reading his mind. "His name is Denedi. In Athabascan, it means luminous or shiny."

"Luminous," Jake repeated softly. Yes, it fit. In the half-light of evening, had the dog been a few feet distant, Jake was sure it would almost have glowed. Earlier he'd been sure the dog was the platinum color of the snow on the Talkeetna slopes; now, as the light overhead dimmed, the dog's coat seemed suffused with an incandescence as well. "I guess what Red Pulaski said is true, huh? About Tanana and Denedi being part wolf?" Until now Jake had not been entirely content to believe that story. It had seemed fanciful, a yarn that might have only a tiny grain of truth to it.

Kamina shrugged. She seemed to be thawing out a little. "All I know is what I've heard from the Old Ones," she answered tersely. "My grandfather caught an almost-white wolf bitch in a trap he'd set for fox over by the Tanana River. The wolf was nearly dead by the time he checked his trapline; her foreleg was mangled and green with infection. But even though he had many other traps to check that day, my grandfather loaded her onto his sled and carried her all the way back to Nyotek."

"She lived through it, huh?"

Kamina gave him a baleful glare. She's not thawed out yet, Jake warned himself. "The shaman in our village—a shaman is a medicine man, in case you don't know it—treated the she-wolf with a poultice made out of secret herbs and wrapped her leg up in birch bark. Later she was mated to a malamute from a village farther up the river. The birth of her pups was too much for her, though. She died, and only one of the pups lived. He was a big, gray-

35

white dog; they say he could drink the wind. He fathered many pups, and two of them were Tanana and Denedi, which means each is one-quarter wolf." Then she shrugged. "The story came down to me from many mouths, and who can say for sure what is true and what is not after so many tellings?"

"True or not, it's a neat story," Jake volunteered. He leaned over to pull affectionately at Skosha's ear. "Skosha, here, she's a good dog, too," he said, "but like Red Pulaski says, probably not good enough to run the Iditarod. Danny used to say speed wasn't such a big thing in a long race, though. He said staying power was what counted most. But I suppose with people coming in from the Outside to run the Big I with fancy crossbreds like Targhee hounds and . . ."

"Speaking of coming in from the Outside," Kamina interrupted him brusquely, "I sure don't know what'd ever give an Outsider the idea that after a few lousy weekends spent behind a bunch of fishburners he was ready to try the Last Great Race. Danny'd been gearing up for the race most of his life." She paused. "Matter of fact, lots of people have."

"Oh, I know for sure I wouldn't win anything," Jake admitted quickly. "Like I told you, it's a gesture. From me to Danny. A way of saying good-bye."

"Well, Outsider, that's what I decided, too."

Jake blinked. It took him a moment to understand exactly what she'd said. "*You're* going to enter the Iditarod?"

"You bet your sweet jingler I am," Kamina snapped, "so you can forget all about taking Danny's team back to town with you. We got other dogs in the village, for sure, but I'm gonna pick 'em over and take the best I can get." Her voice was too loud for a girl, Jake thought. What sort of tender nothings could such a girl be tempted to whisper into the ear of a guy like Bo? Probably something like "Buzz off, turkey!" in decibels that'd do permanent damage to his hearing. Jake also noticed that her fist was still rammed into her pocket. Well, she didn't need to threaten *him* with any knife: He knew when he was licked.

In a way, maybe it was a big relief. Now he could hand over Danny's team, get back to Smalley's, forget all about memorial gestures. He'd go back to a life of pooper-scooping every night and getting a phone call from Dad once a week. Jake peered at the sky. There was still about an hour of daylight left. If he started right away, he could log another six miles before he had to stop to make camp for the night.

"Well, at least you had enough brains to come to the right place for good dogs," Kamina grudgingly admitted. Swell. Now that she's killed off my plans, she wants to be civilized, Jake thought. Forget it, lady. He watched her take her hand out of her pocket. No *ulu,* he noticed. "In my opinion," she went on, her voice softer as she fondled Denedi's muzzle, "this guy's an even better leader than Tanana was. Maybe he's more of a throwback, like me."

She was a lover of the Old Ways, Red Pulaski had said. Terrific, Jake thought, let her hang onto them until they all get moldy, her included. Meantime, he had to get started back to town. He turned on his heel, but Kamina's next words arrested him in midstride.

"Hey, Outsider—as long as you're here, do you want to see the sled I'm going to use in the Iditarod?" she asked. "Danny made it himself. He got it finished about six weeks ago. Tried it out when he came home alone on weekends. Maybe you'd like to have a look at it, since you seem to be hung up on memorial gestures and all that stuff."

Jake shrugged. He could afford ten more minutes. They'd be the last ones he'd ever spend in Nyotek; after today he never planned to set foot in the place again. He wrapped his snub rope around a pole in the Yumiat yard and followed Kamina past the darkened entry of her parents' house. From the willow stick staked nearby, Danny's brilliant scarf moved lightly on the cold January air.

Beyond the snowy mound that marked the Yumiat house was a small building that was not, like the house, half-buried in the earth. It was constructed of birch logs and had been neatly chinked with moss and river mud. The stretched skin of a white Arctic fox was tacked to its door to dry. Strung from poles to the left of the building were several other skins; later, Jake knew, they would be stacked and placed in a cache safe from village dogs and prowling wolverines.

Kamina unlatched the door of the tiny building and pushed it open. "Danny really hated aluminum sleds," she reminded him. "He said he'd rather be hung with a new rope than run a race in a metal sled." She struck a match against the doorjamb and held it to a cotton wick that floated in a shallow dish of oil. In a moment the little room was filled with flickering yellow light, and against the far wall was the most beautiful wooden sled Jake had ever seen.

"Danny called it K'enu," Kamina said quietly. "It means good luck. That's what he was sure he'd have every time he drove it." Jake eased himself forward and touched the driving bow. It had been steamed and molded into the most precise curve, neither too shallow nor too wide. Then it had been wrapped with babiche, or pencil-thin strips of caribou hide. Babiche also webbed the sides of the sled basket. How Danny must've dreamed as he worked on this

thought. But when they stepped outside a moment later, she rolled the hood of her parka into a collar around her neck, and her face once again settled into a hard mask. She peered across the snowfields to the west.

"Look, they're coming home, my parents and all the others," she announced. "Last night, see, we had a stick dance for Danny. You said you wanted to run a race to say goodbye to him; well, *this* is the way of my people. After the stick dance is over, the stick is broken into many small pieces, and in the morning everyone goes to the river to throw them in. I didn't go, though; I had plenty to do right here." Yes, Jake thought, those names on Danny's sled were your way of saying goodbye.

He turned his glance in the direction of Kamina's pointing finger. Two figures, followed by several others, plus all the dogs who hadn't welcomed him into the village an hour before, approached through the pewter-colored winter gloom. "They're hurrying now," Kamina told him, "because the hour of the wolf is coming soon and they want to be safely home."

*The hour of the wolf* . . . Jake had a vision of marauding wolves falling upon the hapless villagers, could hear their screams of fear, saw scarlet stains on the snow. He reached up to cinch the drawstring on the hood of his parka, and his index finger grazed the scar under his ear. There hadn't been any wolves in the glacial whiteness of the emergency room at the County Medical Center, though, so why did he feel that he was once again being tugged back, back into his own past?

Kamina reached out, peeled Danny's scarf from the pole beside the entry to her parents' house, and looped it around her neck. A strand of her hair had loosed itself from the long braid that fell down her back and fluttered

41

against her cheek like a thin, black ribbon. Jake thought of Mibsie, who'd worn a narrow velvet ribbon around her throat the last Christmas he'd spent at home. So long ago, so long. . . . But how had he gotten so far away? What was he doing in this cold, forbidding land he'd never asked to visit? And why was he talking to this angry, black-eyed Athabascan girl about something called the hour of the wolf?

"Danny was going to do it all," Kamina muttered, and Jake realized she was talking more to herself than to him. "He was going to be a winner for all of us. The trouble was, there were two Dannys. One smiled a lot and got his picture in *The Eagle*. The other Danny, the one only a few of us knew, didn't know if he could hack it, be a lawyer and all that fancy stuff he had planned."

A single bead of perspiration, round and perfect as a BB, escaped Jake's armpit and traveled slowly down the ladder of his ribs. He felt another irresistible backward tug and, with a chill, remembered Danny's shrewd, shy we-share-a-secret glance. "Didn't know if he could hack it?" Jake echoed. "What're you talking about, anyway?" He hoped that she would shrug, turn away, be as cross and belligerent as she'd been since they first met.

Instead, Kamina turned to face him. It was too dark now to see her eyes, and Jake fastened his glance instead on the red scarf around her neck. "Haven't you figured it out yet, Outsider?" he heard her ask. Her voice was soft with regret. "My brother Danny killed himself."

# 6

· ·

ON HIS WAY BACK to Smalley's, Jake kept to the trail for four hours, rested for four, ran again for four hours. It was cold, but clear and windless. When he slept he didn't bother to pitch the tent but simply rolled out his sleeping bag and huddled close to Skosha and Benjie. Danny drifted through his restless dreams, at one moment smiling a familiar, brilliant smile, at another moment whispering, *I wonder if I got the kind of juice it'll take to do all the things I want to do.* When Jake woke from such dreams, it was with a pounding heart and an upper lip beaded with cold sweat, and he realized that to believe *he* could run the Iditarod when Danny had such doubts was absurd.

"There were two Dannys," Kamina had said. Jake had hated her then, had hated those words. Now, alone with Skosha and Benjie, he knew Kamina was right. During his last year at home, when he'd dragged himself out of bed in the morning and forced himself to look at the reflection in the bathroom mirror, Jake had known *he* was made up of two halves, too. The person in the glass was quiet, slow, stoic. But if he moved quickly enough he could catch sight of the other one, the scared, resentful one who stood behind the first one. That there were two Jakes was a secret

43

he'd been able to keep to himself until that afternoon at the County Medical Center. Danny'd kept *his* secret from everyone except Kamina until the very end.

Doc Smalley was waiting in the dog-lot behind the animal clinic when Jake mushed in with only a pair of dogs to pull his sled. Take Jake, had been the Mathiessen family chorus; it was my good luck, Jake realized, that it was Win Smalley who agreed to. The doctor stood with two fists the size of hams braced against his hips. His eyes were a pair of bright blue beetles in the glare of the mercury yard light, and he gave Jake a crooked, knowing smile of welcome.

"Well, if it isn't my old buddy, Sergeant Preston of the Yukon. Guess I don't have to ask how you made out on your mission up north, do I?" he asked, eyeing Skosha and Benjie. Jake shook his head and grinned, too. It wasn't a grinning-type predicament, but there was something about the sight of Win Smalley that always made Jake feel there was hope. In most ways, he mused, I know Win better than I ever knew my own Dad, even if a year ago I didn't know a guy by that name existed anywhere on the face of the earth. He'd never heard the name mentioned, in fact, until one afternoon about a week after he got home from the adolescent psych ward at the County Medical Center.

His stay in the trauma unit, recovering from the bullet wound, had been short. The trip to the psych ward was shorter, only three flights up in an elevator. He didn't go alone, of course; two nurses escorted him, one of whom looked as if she could've heaved Win Smalley over her shoulder and won a hundred-yard dash. He went in a wheelchair, even though he pointed out to the nurses there was nothing wrong with his legs.

There were only two other kids in the unit. One sat near a window in the activity room and never spoke. A real

44

airhead. The other guy had a cast on each leg; he'd hurled himself off the Mendota Bridge one night when the river was low and broke both legs when he mired himself to the waist in thick, rich Mississippi River mud. Still, Mother liked to call the time *her* son spent in the unit "convalescing from his accident."

"I tried to kill myself," Jake wanted to remind her. "The word for what I did is suicide. Say it, Mother, s-u-i-c-i-d-e." But to have spelled it out for her like that would've made her feel as bad as getting a pet that didn't coordinate with the new color scheme like it was supposed to.

Besides, nobody else in the family wanted to use that word, either. Mibs kept looking at him with what Jake decided was a mixture of horror and fascination. "Go ahead, Mibsie," he wanted to say, "ask me about it. I'll tell you anything you want to know." She never did, though, and kept away from his room as though she were afraid he might say something she didn't want to hear. Then, three days after he got home, there was a movie on TV about a fourteen-year-old girl who'd tried to do the same thing he had—with pills, though, not a pistol. She got her stomach pumped and didn't die, either. Mother decided it was the very night she just had to spend the entire evening in the apricot living room looking at old family pictures, remembering life like she thought it used to be.

"I think maybe it was the pressure of living in a large metropolitan area that finally got you down," Dad suggested the following week. Large metropolitan area? Why couldn't he just say big city? Jake wondered irritably, and glanced at his watch. It was three o'clock; he'd forgotten to take the tranquilizer the doctor had prescribed. Dad's glance was purposeful, however, and Jake realized belatedly that he hadn't been invited to the backyard, given lemonade, and settled in an umbrella chair for simple fellowship. The occasion had arrived for A Serious Talk.

"But we've never lived anywhere else, Dad," Jake groused. "Minneapolis has always been home. How come you think it's all of a sudden driving me crazy?"

"I wish you hadn't used that word, Jake. You're not crazy. You're just having some problems growing up, that's all. The doctors in that place you stayed after you got out of the trauma unit"—Dad couldn't call it the psych ward, Jake noticed—"they said even your family might be too much pressure for you to handle. So I think a slower-paced, more natural life might be better for you, at least for a while. Something less sophisticated than what you're exposed to here."

"Something more macho?" Jake suggested. There were photographs that covered a whole wall in the den, of Dad at the University in a varsity sweater . . . with a racquet, in tennis whites . . . poised on the end of a diving board in the Olympic tryouts (he'd qualified but had to drop out when he came down with mono—no fault of his, of course). Dad was exactly what a manly man was supposed to be—active, aggressive, and unsuicidal.

"No, that's not what I meant, Jam." *Jam.* That stupid name that's practically shaped what I am, Jake thought wearily. On the one hand, Dad wants me to grow up quicker than I can; on the other, he wants to remind me what a pain in the arse I've always been.

"And as I see it, Jake, the other part of your trouble may be a bad case of bad companions. You just fell in with the wrong crowd the day you got into Simpson High. Maybe it could've happened to anybody. Just because we've been able to live, well, I guess the best word is comfortably, that doesn't mean things can't go haywire. And that Bo you've been hanging out with lately—he's a real loser, Jake. I don't care if his old man *is* on the board of directors at National City Bank. Bo's spoiled, got too many of all the wrong things—his own car, big allowance, no supervision. A bad scene, that's for sure."

And for sure we have been able to live comfortably, Jake thought. He stared across the backyard; it looked like a country club. There was a tennis court at the far end, tidy and black-topped; in the summer Dad played every morning at six with Milt Gunther from next door. The flowers that bordered two sides of the yard were weedless, and the lawn between was as smooth as a piece of green indoor-outdoor carpet. A yard man came twice a week to make sure it stayed that way.

Dad spread five long, brown fingers across each knee. He seemed to have run into a snag in his presentation to the jury. That's the way he approached every conversation, like it was a case he had to win. His face was as tan as his fingers. On top of tennis every morning, he golfed twice a week. He wore tinted aviator glasses that made him look younger than his forty-five years, and his belly was as flat as it'd been in those pictures in the den.

"We could switch you to a private school, Jake. The cost isn't important. That's probably where you should've been all along. But the more your mother and I have talked about it, the more we think you need to get away. I mean, really *away*. Maybe that'd be the best solution of all."

"Away?" Jake shielded his eyes with a visor made of his fingers. Since the accident (how easy it was to think of it that way!) he'd loathed going outdoors. He hadn't walked Mozart around the block once since he'd gotten home. The light was somehow too light, the evenings too melancholy, the smell of trees and grass and flowers always too painful.

"How far away is away, Dad?" He could see it from their point of view, of course—out of sight, out of mind. They could keep calling it the accident and talk about how he was now recovering nicely, poor brave boy, in some far-off, privileged place.

"Well, I've been talking to Win Smalley, Jam. Wouldn't have thought about Win at all except for seeing him at our class reunion this spring. He hasn't changed as much as the rest of us. Of course, Win was always different." Dad rose lightly off his chair, enough to pinch his perfectly pressed white slacks up at the knee so they wouldn't be tempted to bag. His blue blazer with the gold anchor buttons told Jake that later he'd be on his way to join one of his partners on the boat owned by the firm. Dad liked boating, naturally, but said the best part about the *Sally Forth* was that she was a good tax write-off.

Potentially baggy knees eliminated, Dad asked carefully, "Have I ever mentioned Win Smalley to you before, Jake?"

"No, Dad," Jake sighed. Another thing—since he'd got home he was tired all the time. Those pills made it hard to pay attention, hard to care about doing anything except sitting or sleeping. "No, you sure never mentioned Win Smalley to me before, Dad." Also, it was wearisome to have Dad talk to you, around you, past you, but hardly ever to you.

"I called Win last night, Jake. Win's even more of an outdoorsman now than he used to be." Geez, Jake thought, another one. "Win's got himself twenty acres on the outskirts of the town where he lives now." Swell. Jake could feel Dad studying him to see how well the summation was going down. "I think Win told me that his most recent hobby was raising his own dogs. Win didn't marry as soon as the rest of us, Jake, but now he's got a son of his own. Little chap's about two, I think he said. Win's a vet, Jake."

"Which war, Dad?"

"There you go, Jake. That negative, snide attitude is part of your problem, whether you want to admit it or not. Sometimes I get the feeling you don't take very seriously what's happened. Anyway, Win's a veterinarian, not a vet from a war." It's my life, Jake wanted to object, of course I take it seriously. He shut his eyes. The darkness behind his lids was a blessing, like dying was supposed to have been.

"Anyway, Jake, Win told me he'd be happy to have you come and live with him and his wife Nora for a while."

Jake groaned but didn't open his eyes. His fate was being decided again. Two years before he'd been shipped off to the BWCA, the Boundary Waters Canoe Area in northern Minnesota, to attend a camp called Skills for Outdoor Living. Its purpose was to teach city types all about the wilderness and how to cope with physical stress. The second day he fell off the dock and broke his big toe. So much for survival. The next year it was a camp called CompuCorps: you worked on computers all day and practiced linear thinking at night. That was worse.

"Where's this guy Smalley live, Dad?"

"Alaska."

"*Alaska?*" Jake struggled feebly to the surface of his lethargy. "There's enough winter every winter in Minnesota, Dad. I don't really need to be shipped to Alaska so I can freeze my buns all year long."

"I'm sure they have summer sometime in Alaska, Jake, and I think the change will be good for you," Dad assured him. He clamped five brown fingers around Jake's left kneecap. It was the signal the decision had been made and would not be unmade.

"Dad, can I ask you something?"

49

"Certainly, Jake. I'm your father; ask me anything."

"What's it mean when somebody says, 'This kid almost bought the farm'?"

Did Dad pale slightly under his healthy tan? "It's a slang way of saying he almost died, Jake," he answered. "Where'd you hear that, anyway?"

"In the emergency room, Dad." After that there didn't seem to be anything more left to say.

But all that was a year ago. Now Win Smalley asked, puzzled, "Don't the Yumiats keep as many dogs as they used to? I thought for sure you'd come back with enough dogs to . . ."

"Oh, I saw lots of dogs around," Jake said. "None of 'em were in the village when I got there, though." How would he ever find the right words to tell Win about the two Dannys? "Looked to me like there were about thirty dogs in the village," he went on, "and at least twelve or fourteen of them are going to run in the Iditarod, all right, but not in front of my sled."

"No kidding! Somebody else up there gonna enter it?"

"Yeah, a mean freaky female by the name of Kamina Yumiat."

"Well, if that don't beat all!" Win took Skosha out of her harness and turned her into her dog-run. "But I guess it doesn't really surprise me. Women have run it before and done very well, although Kamina seems a little on the young side to be trying it."

"She told me she was a year older than Danny and I guess she figures if he was old enough, she is, too. She's definitely not a lady who lacks confidence," Jake muttered. "What's worse, maybe she's got good reason. That's Red Pulaski's opinion, anyhow, and now that I've met her it's mine, too."

Win lifted up the front end of the loaded sled while Jake took the back end, and together they carried it over the cement apron in front of the driveway and into the garage in order to protect the yellow P-Tex, the polyethylene covering on its runners. "She's confident, all right," he agreed. "By the way, did I ever tell you that Kamina stayed with Nora and me for a couple of days before she left to take the boat for Seattle? Used the room right across the hall from where you're staying now."

Jake grunted and lowered his end of the sled onto the garage floor. "Then you probably know her well enough to know she's got kind of a mean streak, too."

"Gosh, can't say either one of us thought of her that way, Jake." Win lowered the garage door as they stepped out. "The impression we got was that for Kamina to watch some of the ways of her people go down the drain was a real emotional thing. See, she's a proud girl—proud of being Athabascan, proud of being an Insider—which, let's face it, isn't all bad."

Jake shrugged. "All I know is that I'm going to have to hustle up some loaners someplace else, because for sure *she's* not going to give them to me." But to get such dogs and work with them for two months before chute time at Mulcahy Park would be a big order, and as he and Win walked toward the house, where Nora's silhouette could be seen, furry and indistinct through the steamed-over kitchen window, a thin, familiar gray mantle of depression settled over Jake's shoulders.

It was nothing like those depressions he used to get, though. Not one of those crushing black monsters that left him too numb to crawl out of bed in the morning or too blitzed to care if he glimpsed that other Jake in the bathroom mirror, thank God. It was more like the feeling Win Smalley liked to call the blues, a feeling Win claimed practically everybody in the world got at one time or another.

"You're traveling in good company, laddie," Win had assured him with fine Scots fervor. "Abe Lincoln went a few rounds with it. So'd old Sigmund Freud—and Winston Churchill used to call his depressions 'my little black dog.' " Exactly how much did Win know about the trauma unit? Jake often wondered, and was grateful Win had never asked anything about it.

Win walked ahead of Jake into the kitchen, filling the doorframe as he passed through it. No sleek, impersonal chrome and Formica kitchen, this one. Here, instead, was the amber glow of knotty pine and a dining table that'd been made out of the planks from an old freight wagon. The air was fragrant with whatever Nora had been roasting in the oven, and those smells, plus the amber glow of the room, mixed with the knowledge that being blue was no reason for a person to kill himself, made Jake want to reach out and pat Win Smalley between his plaid shoulder blades. He did so, furtively. He'd never patted Dad like that. There was just something about expensive, three-piece silk suits on blade-thin men with silver hair that discouraged such intimacies.

"Well, I know where I can get at least one dog, don't I?" Jake quipped softly. "I'll just whistle up little ol' Blackie and put him into harness!" Dad wouldn't have thought much of that remark, either; he would've figured life wasn't being taken seriously. But Win danced about, light on his feet in spite of his two hundred and fifty pounds, and boxed Jake lightly on the arm. "Atta boy," he approved, a smile in his blue-beetle eyes. "Don't be afraid to put that little sucker to work!"

At supper, over Nora's baked chicken and thick cream

gravy, the topic of Kamina Yumiat surfaced again. "Jake tells me that Danny's sister is back in Nyotek to stay, Nora. Says she plans to enter the Iditarod race herself."

Nora brushed thick, brown bangs away from a forehead that was dewy from her efforts at the stove. She shaped a surprised moue with her lips. "I don't know if that's good news or bad news," she said. "Personally, I thought it'd be a good idea if Kamina stayed in Seattle long enough to get over her mania for leading her whole village back into the nineteenth century. The Old Ways, as she calls them, might be fine, but you can't hold back the future, either."

"Besides which," Jake mumbled around a mouthful of chicken, anxious not to think about what Kamina had told him about Danny, "Seattle might've cured her lousy disposition. She made me feel as welcome in Nyotek as a case of measles on a cruise ship."

"Oh, I can tell you someone who liked her a bunch," Nora grinned. "The Little Prince over there—why, he thought Kamina was the cat's pajamas." She beamed in the direction of the Little Prince, also known as Angus Mc-Donald Smalley, who was busy massaging cream gravy into his hair.

"I don't trust the kid's judgment," Jake objected with a smile. "Just look what he's doing with that delicious gravy, putting it all over his outside instead of his inside." Baby Angus beamed back at his audience and carefully began to paint a layer of gravy over his highchair tray.

This is so weird I don't believe it, Jake thought suddenly. Here I am, yakking like a fool about Angus' judgment and a case of measles on a cruise ship, neither of which has anything to do with anything, because the only thing that really matters is that two days ago Kamina Yumiat told me Danny killed himself. Jake slowly swallowed his last mouthful of potatoes and gravy, then laid his fork carefully alongside his plate. Maybe there'd never be a good time to tell Win and Nora what he knew. Instead of trying to find just the right words, maybe he just ought to let it out.

"Kamina," he began, "she isn't really mean, but . . . up there in Nyotek she told me there were two Dannys. . . . Actually, what she said was that . . . that her brother committed suicide."

The Little Prince was too young to understand what the words meant, but he stopped painting with his gravy and listened, too. Win and Nora stared first at their plates, then at Jake. "Oh, Jake," Nora sighed at last, "nobody wants to talk about it, but, well, sometimes when Athabascan boys come in from the villages like Danny did, they're under a lot of pressure to do well, and sometimes the adjustments are harder to make than they look on the outside. We suspected what'd happened to Danny, but there just didn't seem to be any good way to let you know. . . ."

Upstairs, after the supper dishes had been done, Jake stretched out under Nora's patchwork quilt, then reached up to pull his fingers wearily through his hair. Even in the dark, it felt pale and wimpy. He flexed his toes. Sometimes the little black dog slept at the end of his bed. Tonight, though, the dark beast seemed as big as a St. Bernard and made the bed top a bit to one side. Jake closed his eyes against the greenish glow of the yard light outside his window and finally drifted uneasily to sleep.

He woke early, startled, his heart hammering loudly in his chest. He listened, amazed by what he heard. The whole thing *had* been a dream! Danny was back, and the dog-lot was once again full of barking, whining, howling dogs. Confirmation came a moment later when a sleepy Win Smalley called up the stairs, "We've got company, Jake. I think you'd better get down here!"

Jake threw off Nora's quilt and staggered to the window. Frost had made maps of exotic countries on the panes; he raised the sash to see better what was going on below. The back yard was, indeed, full of dogs—huskies of copper, gray, black, white, and several shades in between—hitched to a slim, handmade golden sled, and leaning insolently across its driving bow was an individual Jake had hoped never to lay eyes on again.

Kamina Yumiat glanced up at him, and Jake was astonished to see the tiniest of smiles on her smooth, dark face. "I thought a lot about what you said, Outsider," she called to him over the racket made by the dogs. "About doing something for Danny and memorial gestures and all that junk. So I brought you some dogs for your team." Her smile widened, and Jake could not decide whether it was from mirth or malice. Her next words convinced him it was the latter. "But come chute time," she warned, "I aim to race your socks off, Outsider."

# 7

B Y T H E T I M E Jake got downstairs and out to the
dog-lot, Kamina had already wrapped her snub
rope around a corner of Smalley's fence and was
unsnapping her big, gray lead dog from his position at the
front of the team. "You must've run all night to get here at
this hour," Jake muttered. Was the light in Anchorage
different from the light in Nyotek? Or was it just the soft
glow of the morning sky that made Kamina seem not quite
as sturdy or nearly as fierce as he'd remembered?

The smile she threw in his direction wasn't exactly one
of Danny's toothy versions, but it hinted at a certain agreeableness that forty-eight hours before Jake would not have
thought she possessed. "Denedi's part wolf, remember?"
Kamina reminded him. "Wolves like to run at night, in
case you didn't know. It's in their nature." Jake could also
see that the sight of Denedi had an intimidating effect on
all the dogs Win was boarding. Instead of yapping up a
storm, each watched the wolf-dog with cautious respect.

Jake studied the thirteen dogs still hitched to Kamina's
sled. "Do I get to pick which ones I want?" he teased nervously.

"Not exactly, Outsider. I'm taking Denedi and this
ginger-colored dog back with me. You get what's left.
Those who make deals for loaners, see, take whatever they
can get." Jake noticed that *he* got Sundance, good old sass

and flash himself. Kamina slipped Denedi out of his harness and chained him by his leather collar to one of the stakes in the dog-lot that used to be Danny's. "By the way, does Doc Smalley know yet that you want to run the Big I?"

Jake was about to answer when the back door slammed and Nora came out, a heavy sheepskin coat thrown over her nightclothes, the Little Prince riding on her hip. "Kamina," she exclaimed, "is our new boarder the only reason you'll come back to visit us anymore?" Nora slyly poked an elbow in Jake's ribs, and to his amazement, Kamina Yumiat, the terror of Seattle, blushed like an ordinary schoolgirl.

"I'm sorry, Mrs. Smalley, for waiting so long to thank you for the letter you sent my parents after Danny . . . after he died. I read it to them; they'd like to thank you, too."

Nora was instantly contrite. "Hey, Kamina, I was only teasing. I know how much all of you've had on your minds lately. But here—here's a little guy you made quite an impression on! How about that, Angus?" As soon as he felt all eyes turn in his direction, the Little Prince tried to burrow into his mother's armpit. "This is his invisible act," Nora whispered loudly. "He thinks if he can't see you, then you can't see him either!"

Kamina reached out to tug on the toe of Angus's sleepers. Angus gave a happy squeal and held his arms out to her. Jake watched as Kamina kissed the baby and hugged him hard. Bo isn't the only one who's comfortable with girls, Jake thought. Even Angus can handle 'em. I'm the only one who doesn't know how to act or what to say. When Angus began to shiver, Nora retrieved him, stuck him back inside her coat, and ordered with a smile, "Stake your team, Kamina, and come on in for breakfast."

"Gosh, I didn't come down to freeload off you again,

Mrs. Smalley. I'll just let the dogs rest a couple hours and then I'll . . ."

"Last time you were here you promised to call me Nora, remember? And of course you'll have breakfast, and stay with us overnight besides. Jake, help Kamina unhitch, and I'll go in to start some pancakes."

As soon as he found himself alone with Kamina again, Jake started to shift nervously from one foot to the other. He looked everywhere except right at her. If she stayed all day, didn't leave until tomorrow morning, what'd they ever find to talk about? A second later he realized he shouldn't have worried; Kamina would take care of the conversation.

"Well?" she snapped. "I thought you said you were Danny's handler—so handle!"

Jake flushed. "Okay, okay! The doc's got a couple of empty pens, so if you want to . . ."

"Better put the two who'll be going home with me out here on stake chains," Kamina said. "If you want to put *your* dogs in pens—and I use the possessive pronoun only temporarily—that's up to you." She deftly slipped her second lead dog out of harness and fastened it to a stake in the dog-lot.

"Now, that copper-colored team dog right beside you there is a darned good dog," Kamina went on. "You'll never get any trouble from her, but that wheel dog over there to the left—he's part hound, and I call him Blue Jeans on account of he's just about that color—he's a good hauler but he'll probably give you fits. Danny got him from a dog-lot up near Huslia, and he's a natural-born loner. He might even show you some teeth."

"Show me some teeth?"

"Yeah. You know, snarl at you, make a pass at your

58

wrist. Don't take any sass off him, though. You shouldn't be mean to a dog like that, but you sure gotta be firm!" Jake screwed a firm look on his face and reached to unsnap Blue Jeans from his place on the gangline. Sure enough, the big blue dog turned, curled his lip, and left two ribbons of broken skin on Jake's wrist as a get-acquainted souvenir.

Jake decided later that Kamina must've had her eye on both of them the whole time, for she stepped quickly across the gangline, seized Blue Jeans by his collar and the tail-end of his harness, lifted him bodily off the ground, and gave him three vigorous shakes. She set him back on his feet with an emphatic thunk.

"There's nothing in the world a dog hates worse than being held off the ground like that," she explained. "But you gotta discipline a dog like Blue Jeans the minute he cuts up; otherwise, he doesn't know what he's catching the devil for. Me and Danny never whup our dogs, though. That'd make 'em shy and hate to run for you, which sure ain't the name of the racing game."

Jake knew that if he shut his eyes, it'd be Danny he heard talking, not Kamina, telling him things it'd take years to learn on his own. It was plain that any time spent around Kamina would be as well spent as the hours he'd spent with Danny. It'd be dumb to make a move on her, though—that's what Bo called it when he wanted to get something from a girl. Bo probably didn't have dogsled-racing lessons in mind, however.

Jake cleared his throat and hoped he sounded natural. "Hey, it'd be neat if you decided to stay overnight, Kamina. I bet the Little Prince'd sure hate to see you leave again so soon."

Kamina arched a surprised black eyebrow in his direction. "*The Little Prince?* Is *that* what you call yourself?"

Jake wanted to chew his knuckles. She was a tough lady to fool. That's the price you pay for acting smart, Mathiessen, he told himself. "Angus—*Angus* is the Little Prince. Win and Nora got the name from some book they like real well. But . . . well, I'd like you to stay, too. Maybe we could, you know, talk."

"Talk? About what?"

"The race. What happened to Danny. Stuff."

Kamina gave him a quick, suspicious look. "Naw. I got lots to do back in the village. The purse in the Iditarod is gonna be a hundred thou this year, and they pay for the first twenty finishers. Even if I run seventeenth or eighteenth, it'd still mean more'n a thousand dollars. I got lots of training to do, Outsider—and *you* better start thinking that way, too."

"You want to hear something funny?" Jake blurted.

"Not especially, but I got a feeling you're gonna tell me anyhow."

"Well, when I first met you I figured maybe you didn't understand English very well. That's how dumb I am."

"That's how dumb, all right," Kamina agreed. But when she turned to face him, Jake saw a sly smile turn up the corners of her mouth. Even more surprising, he saw a dimple in her cheek. As girls went, she wasn't the worst-looking one he'd ever seen; Bo might even let her out on a few nights other than Halloween.

Later, over stacks of super-sized pancakes, wedges of smoked ham, and mountains of scrambled eggs, Jake decided he'd better enlist Nora's help. "Kamina says she can't stay overnight after all," he mumbled innocently around a mouthful of food. Nora looked as dismayed as he'd hoped she would.

"I just won't hear another word about it!" she exclaimed in mock outrage. "You have to stay overnight, Kamina. I've got a nifty macrame I've been working on and I remember how much help you gave me with my knots last time, just before you took the boat for Seattle."

"Gee, I really don't think I should, Mrs. Sm—Nora, I mean. But I'd sure like a few more hotcakes. . . ." Nora started to pass the plate to Kamina, then held it back with a smile. "Promise you'll stay? Promise?" Kamina rolled her black eyes. "Okay, okay—but only one night." She sent a stern look across the table. "Some people might be armchair racers, but that's not how we train in Nyotek!"

She fell into it, Jake thought smugly. He'd made a move on her; Bo would be proud. "Talk about racing," he murmured, "how about you and me dividing up the number of dogs we got out there in the lot and doing a little racing tomorrow before you go home?"

Kamina narrowed her eyes speculatively. She's as interested in taking my measure as I am in learning everything she knows, Jake realized. "Sure, Outsider," she agreed softly. "Can't be any harm in a little race. Might even be fun." Fun was not what she had on her mind, he knew. She pulled thoughtfully at the single long, black braid that hung over her left shoulder and added in a whisper, "We might as well try to be civilized a little while longer, on account of in a few more weeks it's gonna be you against me, and me against you."

"You plan to use that black-and-white husky—what'd you call her, Skosha?—in the lead?" Kamina wanted to know the next morning.

"I guess so," Jake answered. "Number one, she's the best I've got, and number two, she does pretty good. You got

61

that wolf mutt, so you'll race the socks off me, if I recall your words right."

"Denedi's not a mutt, but you're right about the socks part. Anyway, we got a total of fourteen dogs between us, counting your two, my two that're going back to Nyotek, and the ten I'm loaning to you. So, for the race, you take eight so you can run a double leader. I'll take the six that're left because Denedi's practically a whole team by himself, anyway. Fair?"

"Fair. Only who'll I run in the lead alongside Skosha?"

"How about that little copper-colored bitch? She's had some lead training. 'Course, it'd be better if one of 'em was a male; usually it's better to pair up opposite-sex dogs, but in a pinch we can't be choosy."

Win helped hold the teams while they hitched, and Nora kibitzed from the kitchen window. "You want to run out toward the mountains where Danny and I used to train?" Jake asked.

Kamina glanced toward the Chugach range that provides a stunning backdrop for the city of Anchorage. Her face was a mask Jake could not see behind, and he wished he'd suggested someplace else. "We don't have to go that way," he added quickly. "There's lots of places we could go if . . ."

"Forget it, okay? What happened, happened," she snapped.

Win drove behind them in the station wagon, carefully straddling the sled trail with the car wheels so that he wouldn't mess up the nicely groomed trail that Danny and Jake had worked on since November. After they got to the starting point, Win hauled a stopwatch out of his pocket. "Who goes first?" he wanted to know. "Beauty or brains?"

By then Kamina had recovered enough to shrug and say,

"That way we'd both lose. Besides, we're racing the clock, not each other." She jerked a thumb in Jake's direction. "But I'll go first to give this *cheechako* something to run after."

The training loop Danny had made covered a five-mile course. Sometimes he ran it starting from the right side, sometimes from the left, because it bored the dogs to run exactly the same way every session. The trick was, he advised Jake, to always run the dogs away from their starting point; to run them back and forth past that point was bad psychology and didn't help them develop a good running attitude.

Kamina checked her lines, got her team in place, and when Win hollered "H*iiiiii*ke!" Denedi, who was already leaning into his harness, leaped out with flattened ears and a mile-eating stride. Kamina gave several hard pedaling motions, following each pedal with a wide upward arc so that there was no backward jerk against the dogs' forward movement. She had a jingler like the one Danny had made, and when she flicked it, Jake saw the rest of her team flatten their ears and settle into a hard sprint.

Skosha looked back at Jake from her place in the left lead. "Don't look at me like that, babe!" Jake pleaded. "We'll just have to do our best, that's all."

"Ready, Sergeant Preston?" Win laughed. Jake nodded, but when Win hollered "H*iiiiii*ke!" again, Blue Jeans leaned so hard into his harness and gave the sled such a mighty pull that he almost dumped Jake on his head. Jake hung onto the driving bow and thought well, so much for the well-pedaled start.

Because of the way the training trail had been carved, Jake could keep Kamina in profile most of the time. She crouched low, he noticed, and didn't so much hang onto her driving bow as kneel behind it. Whenever the sled hit a bump on the trail, she shifted her weight expertly so that no backward jerk was passed through the bridle of the sled to the racing dogs. Keep things smooth and even, Danny used to say. Kamina seemed to have learned that lesson very well.

Jake was so busy watching her that he didn't see the tree branch sticking out of the snow ahead of him. It caught the edge of his right runner and the sled bounced and slid hard into Blue Jeans' hindquarters. "Sorry, pooch," Jake apologized. "I'll try to pay more attention next time."

When Kamina was at the farthest end of the training loop, Jake saw her begin to drive hard for the finish line. The distance that now separated the two sleds was much greater than it'd been at the beginning of the race, Jake observed without surprise. "Maybe that's why I never liked girls," he muttered. "They're just too tough!" Mibsie'd been tough, too, in her sweet, silky way. "If you don't like how Dad treats you, Jake, *tell* him," she'd advised him once. "*I* would," she'd added. Somehow, Jake never could.

By the time he got back to Win's station wagon, Jake knew he must be at least ten or twelve minutes behind Kamina's time. "How bad did I do?" he asked. "Better ask how well Kamina did," Win suggested. "She did the five-mile course in twenty-six minutes, or close to eleven miles an hour. Not too shabby, huh?"

"Not too shabby," Jake agreed. "How about me?"

"Let's see—it took you forty-four minutes to cover the same ground, which means you were ticking along at about seven miles an hour. You'll really need to practice, kid, if you aim to luck out in those sprint races. I've clocked some of those guys at sixteen miles an hour, Sergeant Preston."

Of course Win doesn't know that sprint races are not my concern, Jake thought. And the news that he'd only done seven miles an hour didn't sound as grim to him as it did to Win. A steady, reliable eight miles an hour was the figure Danny had been aiming for for the Iditarod. Jake felt Kamina's eyes search his own. I hope she doesn't spill the beans, he thought. He held her glance with his own and was relieved when she only smiled and shrugged and let him keep the news about the Big I to himself.

Clad in a pair of baggy white long johns, Win Smalley looked like a sleepy, red-headed polar bear when Jake found him in the kitchen pouring coffee the next morning. Kamina was long gone, and Jake was glad it was Sunday, the only morning of the week Nora slept late.

"Want a shot of wake-up juice, kid?" Win asked with a wide, bearish yawn. "It's been on the back of the stove all night; by now it oughta float nails." Jake nodded and reached for some cream. He took a swallow, blinked, and leaned across the steam from his coffee cup. There'd never be a better time to tell Win what he planned to do.

"Kamina didn't exactly bring those dogs down from Nyotek just to make me feel better after the bad time she gave me up there," he said. He checked Win's bearded face for surprise.

The doctor merely looked groggy. "I guess I don't get your drift, Jake," he admitted. "I figured you wanted to try a little sprint racing, and that's why you were looking for some loaners. To see how you liked the sport and all that."

"Actually, I *am* interested in racing," Jake confessed. "And what I thought I'd do is . . . enter the Iditarod."

Win Smalley gasped, choked, recovered with red, watery

65

eyes. "The *Iditarod?* Ah, laddie, your first Alaska winter has softened up your brain! The Big I isn't a polite little sprint race like the ones Danny let you try when he felt like flirting with some girl instead of running them himself! And Danny'd probably been saving the entry fee for years. It's more than a thousand dollars, in case you don't know—a thousand for the length of the race, with forty-nine tacked on to testify that Alaska's the forty-ninth state."

Win paused for breath and went on. "And if the expense of entering isn't enough for you, you've got school and all your chores here at the hospital. Not to mention there's only a shade over two months left before chute time at Mulcahy Park. Most guys have been training for at least six, which leaves you way behind before you even start."

"My dad sends me an allowance, on top of what he pays you and Nora for my board and room," Jake said, trying to take one point at a time. "And I can get a leave of absence from school, just like Danny planned to do."

Win frowned. "Another hangup will be getting your entry form validated, Jake. See, a rookie racer is obliged to have two signatures on his application from someone active in the sport or from a sanctioned dog club. Danny belonged to a club, plus he was well-known from his competition in all those village races. He was legit, Jake, no question about it. As for someone active in the sport signing for *you* . . ."

"You've been active in it, been a steward and all that," Jake reminded him. "You could sign for me."

Win settled his polar bear body more firmly into his kitchen chair. He turned his coffee cup slowly around in his thick fingers and studied Jake unhappily. Win had never asked a word about what'd happened in Minnesota.

Until now Jake was glad the subject had never been mentioned. Entering the Iditarod changed all that.

"You're thinking about why my dad sent me up here in the first place, right?" Jake asked. "I suppose he told you that I . . . that I tried to. . . ." Mother wasn't the only one who had trouble saying the word. "That I tried to commit suicide with my great-grandfather's pistol. It was old; I found it in the attic one afternoon. I went up there mainly to get away from the rest of the family. It was peaceful, nothing around but old clothes and boxes of pictures. And my great-grandfather's pistol. I hid it behind some books on my bookshelf for six months before I worked up enough nerve to use it."

"Yes, Jake, your dad told me," Win admitted quietly. "He talked about it the first time he called me. He was pretty unglued over the whole thing." Dad, unglued? It sure hadn't showed; he'd been calm throughout the whole affair. Mother and Mibsie were the ones who acted like the world had come apart, and every time they came to the trauma unit they looked like they'd been crying for a week. "I know you think all that is in the past, Jake, and that you could never feel that way again, but I . . ."

"What happened to Danny makes everything different, Win. I know Danny never meant for Tanana to drown, too. Danny headed for that overflow hole alone, but Tanana tried to pull him back. That's when both of 'em ended up going under. If Danny could do it all over again, I know he'd make a different decision. Because after I got up here with you and Nora, that's how it was for me. And about the Iditarod, well, I *have* to run it, Win. I told Kamina I wanted to do it for Danny. What I meant was, it's for me, too."

Win wagged his curly red bear's head back and forth.

67

"Oh, laddie, laddie! Surely you remember how fierce last winter was! Out on the trail it's going to be even worse. You'll be crossing the Alaska Range about the fifth day of the race and you'll go down the other side into the Interior, where really bad winters are born and bred. Add onto the weather some other problems a musher faces—fatigue, lame dogs, broken sleds, wrong turns taken, dehydration—and what've you got? A potential nightmare, that's what. Some guys who've run it have come home talking about the hallucinations they've had on the trail, brought on by all the stresses they've faced. They've said they saw ghosts, strange lights, villages that weren't there." Win fixed Jake with a piercing blue gaze. "Besides, Jake, you need *two* signers. If I sign, where'll you come up with somebody equally as daft as I think I might be getting ready to be?"

Jake grinned. "I think Red Pulaski might sign for me. When we went out to look at the overflow hole, he said, 'Dreams die hard.' It made me think he'd understand what I want to do." Jake swallowed the last dregs of his cup of floating nails and stood up. Outside, the sun was coming over the Chugach Mountains and had turned the frost on the window above the sink into orange cake icing. After he'd rinsed his cup, Jake scratched a peephole in the frost with his thumbnail and peered through it with one eye. Skosha was standing on top of her kennel, her front paws braced against the wire fence, studying the trail Kamina had taken back to Nyotek. She looked exactly like somebody's favorite lead dog, Jake thought.

Win lumbered across the kitchen and laid a heavy paw across Jake's shoulder. "Well, I guess Nora'd better start stitching up some booties, huh?" He yawned.

Jake flushed. "Booties?" he echoed. "I'm going to run a race, not become a father."

"Ah, I can see you've got a lot to learn." Win sighed. "Race rules say each musher has to carry two pair of booties for each dog on his team. You'll be starting the race with twelve dogs, which means forty-eight feeties, or ninety-six booties. And I reckon Nora'd better start baking up a batch of survival brownies, too."

"Yuk. Health-type food never turned me on."

"She makes 'em out of walnuts, coconut, honey, brown sugar, dates, and raisins, all bound together with whole wheat flour. Quick and easy to eat, and they'll give you lots of energy." Win sighed again and padded back toward his bedroom.

"And I got a hunch you might even win the Red Lantern Award."

"The Red Lantern Award?"

"Yup. Given to the guy who crosses the finish line last. You see, this race is so tough that just to finish it is a noble distinction."

There was one minor detail that Jake had still not resolved in his own mind, however. "How, exactly, does a guy find his way to Nome?" he asked. "I'm not sure how to get there, let alone finish last."

Win smiled. "At this very moment, you'll be happy to hear, a bunch of guys are getting ready to go out on snow machines to cut a pathway for you all the way to that distant metropolis. They'll even mark it with pink plastic surveyor's tape for you. All you gotta do is follow the trail —unless, of course, you want to change your mind. . . ."

Jake turned to peer out his peephole again. What was Kamina thinking now? he wondered. "No," he answered softly, "I'm ready to try it. For Danny." And a kid named Jam, he added to himself.

# 8

RED PULASKI scrutinized Jake shrewdly over the
top of a pair of silver reading glasses. "I sure don't
know what you think the Last Great Race is, sonny,
but a lemonade-and-ladyfingers party I assure you it ain't,"
he observed. "Now, I hear your old man's some kinda fancy
lawyer down there in Minnesota; my advice is to have him
represent you at your sanity hearing. Meantime, why don't
you just pack your fanny back out there to Doc Smalley's,
take two aspirin, and hope this attack of lunacy passes?"

"I know how it must sound to you, Mr. Pulaski," Jake
persisted, "but like I said, I already got one signature and
if you will just sign ..."

"Who, if I may be so bold, was foolish enough to put his
John Henry on that entry form?"

"Doc Smalley." Jake grinned in spite of himself.

Red Pulaski rested his forehead on the glass counter in
front of him and heaved a sigh. "It figures," he moaned. "I
suppose if Doc Smalley thought enough of you to invite
you up here to God's country to finish your last two years
of high school, then he'd think enough of you to sign for
you, too." Then Red raised his head from the counter and
skewered Jake on the end of a hard glance. "You a senior
in school, just like Danny was?" he demanded. "On account of you gotta be eighteen to be eligible to enter the
Iditarod."

He's hoping I won't qualify because I'm too young, Jake realized. "I'm not a senior," he admitted, "but I'm eighteen, all right. I was . . . see, I was sick for a year back home and had to repeat a grade."

"Sick?" Did Red sound unduly suspicious? "Yeah," Jake nodded as healthily as he could. "I was in the hospital for a while. Nothing really serious. I'm okay now."

"Sick or well, kid, that don't alter the fact you're a greenhorn. Out in the villages there are boys who've been running behind fishburners since they were tall enough to grab onto a driving bow, just like Danny. I don't have any quarrel with one of them young fellas entering the Iditarod, but you. . . ." Red pulled reflectively at his wisp of brown beard. "See, Jake, it takes a certain kind of personality to face a thousand miles of race, not to mention you should have lots of trail experience. A loner, that's what it takes, Jake. You're a city kid, used to city living. I bet you don't hardly know what it means to be really alone."

That's what I've been all my life, Jake wanted to explain, a real loner. Even when Bo and I were supposed to be such buddies, I was alone. Locked inside my own head. Worried that I wasn't tall enough, good enough, fast enough, enough of anything. And Danny might be here this minute if I'd been able to let him see what I really was, instead of pretending to be something I wasn't. Jake inched the pen across the counter toward Red's stubby fingers.

"I see none of the discouraging words I've laid on you have changed your mind," Red observed mournfully. "You say your insurance is all paid up?"

"Sure." Jake tried to sound cocky. "I'm worth more dead than alive." Once he'd been sure it was true.

Red eyed the pen that was now inches from his grasp. "Providing I completely take leave of my good sense and sign this here piece of paper, what do you aim to do about a sled? Use that crummy aluminum egg crate I loaned you and saw you steering around Smalley's place the other morning when I drove by?"

"Not if I can help it. I figured I'd try to pick up something better secondhand. Unless you've got a better idea."

Red waved casually toward the back of the shop. "You must be doing something right, kid, because a guy came in here about a week ago and dropped off his buggy. Seems like life on the Inside got too tough for him and he was headed back to breathe deeply of that famous L.A. smog. Sled's got a busted stanchion and the P-Tex is all worn off the runners. I think he must've raced it on gravel roads. I reckon I could let you steal it from me for a couple hundred bucks. If you got that kinda cash, that is."

Jake nodded. "My old man gives me an allowance." Dad would take a dim view of being called *my old man*. "I never spend much of it, though. I just salt it away."

"Got no girl to use it on, huh?" Red asked slyly, eyebrows arched over his silver glasses.

Jake flushed. "Well, I did," he lied carefully, "but she decided she liked some other guy better than me."

"So. You got money for a sled; that much is settled. You aim to buy all the rest of your gear right now, or wait to see if you chicken out after all?"

I've already got dogs, a sled, a sleeping bag, a tent, and a Coleman stove, Jake thought. What else do I need? "You gotta pack survival gear," Red intoned patiently, "which includes an ax, snowshoes, two pounds of food per dog per day, a dog bag for injured pooches, some kind of headlamp for night running, and extra batteries to power it. As if that isn't enough, you gotta pack extra hooks for your lines, light tools, P-Tex so you can mend worn runners, changes of clothes for yourself, and your own food—all of which can add up to three hundred pounds or more." In spite of the length of the list, Red wasn't quite through. "Then, of course, you gotta get your drop packages ready by the end of next month—food for you and the dogs that'll be dropped off at the various checkpoints so you don't have to haul it the whole thousand miles yourself."

Ticked off like that it all sounded a bit too real. Jake swallowed, looked down at the pen on the counter, and banished from his mind the suspicion that he might, indeed, be getting in over his head. "It's all academic if I can't get you to make your X on the dotted line at the bottom of this entry form," he insisted.

Red favored him with a final, gloomy look, then wetted the pen against the tip of his tongue. "Maybe *I'm* the one who needs two aspirin and a good lawyer," he muttered as he carefully signed the racing blank.

After Red helped him load the sled into the station wagon he'd borrowed from Win, Jake drove to the post office. He wrote out a check for one thousand and forty-nine dollars. One thing for sure, Dad had never been stingy when it came to money. A check for one hundred and fifty dollars arrived in the mail promptly on the fifth of every month. Jake got a stamp out of a machine and dropped the sealed application into a mail slot beside the door. As he drove back to the animal clinic, he could see the sled in the rearview mirror. He pulled himself up a little straighter behind the steering wheel. Tomorrow, in shop class, he'd begin to make a new stanchion; later Win would help him glue new P-Tex onto the sled runners.

The next time Jake glanced in the mirror, it was his own eyes he caught sight of rather than the silhouette of the sled. They did not, somehow, look like the eyes of a boy who'd once tried to blow his brains out. Jake studied the road ahead, surprised. Maybe that kid was gone. Maybe he was.

Jake stopped riding the bus home at two o'clock every afternoon and began to jog the four miles from the high school to the Smalley Animal Clinic. "Dogs ain't the only mutts that gotta be tough in the Iditarod," Red Pulaski had warned. The first week Jake's lungs felt like they'd burst before he got home, and the calves of his legs ached so bad he could hardly sleep at night. The second week wasn't quite as bad. By the third week he didn't have to stop and rest once in the whole four miles.

As soon as he trotted into the yard every afternoon, the dogs commenced a gleeful chorus, knowing that a training session was at hand. Except for Blue Jeans, there wasn't a sour dog in the bunch, Jake thought, pleased. And huskies could really talk, he decided—not so much by barking as by wailing, howling, groaning, moaning—a mixture of sounds that usually ended on a high, wolfish *AAAAAeeeeee-OOOOOiiiii!* that had the power to send ripples up his spine.

After he'd gobbled down a half-dozen of Nora's cookies and inhaled two glasses of milk, Jake hung Doc's stopwatch around his neck and hustled out to the dog-lot to hitch up. Even after two weeks of running the team, however, Blue Jeans still had to be left till the very last.

"Somehow, pooch, you and me are gonna have to reach an understanding," Jake muttered as he unhooked the blue hound from his stake chain. "Maybe we ought to start off fresh by giving you a new name. B.J.—how'd that suit you? It'd sure be a lot easier to say." He peered hopefully at the hound. B.J., who didn't recognize his new name, studied Jake with hard, yellow, unforgiving eyes. When Jake hauled the blue dog toward his place on the gangline, B.J. snapped halfheartedly, closing his teeth on air.

"That dog just likes to keep his distance from people," Kamina had said. Jake glanced down the gangline to where Skosha and Sissy, the copper bitch, waited in the lead. "So you like to stay your distance from folks, huh?" Jake asked. "Well, mutt, maybe you belong way up there, in the lead." Wasn't it just what Win advised, after all? To keep switching the dogs around to different positions on the team to see where they ran best?

Skosha moved warily to one side as Jake snapped the blue stranger to the gangline beside her. But would Sissy be bent out of shape to see she'd lost her place at the head of the team? Jake breathed a sigh of relief when the little red dog trotted back to B.J.'s place with a good-natured, ho-hum attitude. Whenever he'd run with Danny, Jake had jumped into the sled basket to add extra weight; now with nobody to do the same for him, he hooked a couple of tires to the snub rope and dragged them along behind to make sure the dogs had something to work against.

"Okay, troops, let's move out!" he called cheerfully when he was ready to go. Skosha turned and gave him a disgusted glance. "Sorry," Jake apologized. Skosha was like Mother; she went by the book. "Hiiiiiike!" he hollered instead, and Skosha leaned immediately into her harness. Jake watched, pleased, as B.J. leaned with her.

Instead of following the trail toward the Chugach Mountains, Jake ran north on a little-used county road. When it intersected with another narrow road, he called out sharply, "Haw! Haw!" Without missing a stride, Skosha bent to the left. The swing dogs, Bunkie and Lita, followed; then the wheel dogs guided the sled neatly around the corner. At another intersection he called "Gee! Gee!" and Skosha dove to the right. Even more gratifying than Skosha's growing skill, however, was the way B.J. followed her lead. Maybe he's just a dog who picks things up real quick, Jake thought. On the other hand, maybe he's like me, somebody who'd never found his place, only now he has.

Jake didn't press the team to run as if their tails were on fire. The Big I was an endurance race, a marathon of dog racing, not a sixteen-mile sprinter. What the team needed, he knew, was a chance to develop its lung capacity, its staying power, its ability to hold a steady trot mile after mile. Tomorrow they'd all rest, himself included. It was one more thing he'd learned from Danny: "Dogs get bored, just like you and me," Danny had said. "You can't run 'em seven days a week, week after week. They gotta have a day off now and then, just like we need to break our routine once in a while."

It was dark by the time Jake careened into the dog-lot behind the clinic. He snatched up the stopwatch that dangled around his neck and peered at it in the orange glow cast by Nora's kitchen window. He grinned. He'd been running a steady six miles an hour with Skosha and Sissy up front; it hadn't really been fast enough to be competitive. Now, with B.J. in the lead, they were doing a shade over eight. "Okay, buddy," Jake called softly to the blue hound, "I think you just got yourself a job." B.J. turned, and Jake was not surprised to see that the dog's eyes were as hard and baleful as ever. Maybe he's like Dad and just won't ever warm up to me, Jake thought. Maybe he won't, ever.

The remainder of January and half of February passed in a haze of afternoons spent on the training trails and evenings spent cleaning up the dog-lot, mixing food for the team, and doing chores for the dogs that were boarding. On one such evening Win came out to feel each race team member's backbone, chest, ribs. "They could stand a little more meat on 'em, Jake," he allowed. "Not too much, or they'll feel sluggish and won't run well. On the other hand, they need something to use up on the trail. If they don't have a supply of fat to use, they'll start metabolizing muscle mass, and then you'll be in deep trouble. I think we better start feeding them a mash with plenty of supplements in it, lots of vitamins, fish oil, some bone meal."

"I can mix it up for you, Jake," Nora offered over supper. She pushed her thick brown bangs out of her eyes. "It'll save you time so you won't have to do your homework when you're so pooped you can't see straight."

Jake shook his head. Angus, who wanted to be a part of everything, shook his, too. "I might as well learn how to do it myself," Jake answered. "I'm gonna be tired on the trail, too, and there'll be no one to lend a hand out there." The truth was nobody would be allowed to help him on the trail. Jake had read the race rules so often he knew most of them by heart, and number thirty-four read: "All care and feeding of dogs between checkpoints will be done by the musher only. No planned help is allowed throughout the race. At noncheck points a musher may accept hospitality for himself only." That meant there'd be some free meals and warm beds in a few of the villages they'd pass through on the way to Nome, but the dogs' care would be his responsibility, and his alone.

Nora showed Jake how to cook up the kind of hot mash Win had in mind. In a five-gallon pot he boiled stew meat and liver cut into one-inch cubes. After thirty minutes he added enough raw rice to allow each dog two cupfuls when

77

it'd been cooked. When the rice had cooked enough to absorb most of the meat juices, he added fish oil, honey, wheat germ, vitamins, and bone meal. Jake spooned two cups of mash onto each dog's pie plate and let the mixture cool until it was warm but not hot. After the dogs had eaten, he washed the tins and cooking pot and put them in a corner of the kitchen until next mealtime.

Water was just as important to racing dogs as their food, and following Danny's advice, Jake made sure it was always lukewarm and flavored with a chunk of meat or fish. "Dehydration can put a team down faster than poor food or bad weather," Win warned. "Some guys used to intubate their dogs—run a plastic tube down the dog's mouth into his stomach and force water on the poor mutt. That's against race rules now and always should've been, but it shows how seriously a musher took the fact that his team was doing poorly because of lack of water."

Two weeks later Win checked the dogs again. "They look great, Jake," he announced. "C'mere. I'll show you how to tell if they're just about fat enough." Win ran his fingers down Skosha's side, gently pinching up some skin. It filled his fingers to the width of an inch. "That's like extra gasoline in the tank, kid. Not only do dogs need fat to run on, they need it to keep warm, too. When you're out on the trail, try to let the dogs rest in a warm place—on a sunny snowbank, for instance—so they don't have to use up calories trying to keep warm. If it's a gray day or the wind is blowing hard, rest 'em in the lee side of some brush or rocks. They'll thank you for it."

That night Jake diagrammed all his hook-up possibilities. Except for Skosha and B.J., some of the dogs might do better running in different spots. Bunkie and Lita were in the swing position; maybe tomorrow he'd run them both in a team spot and move Herb and Lefty up behind the leaders. Jake felt like a football coach diagramming plays for Saturday's game. Sundance really ought to stay in the wheel slot, though, just to be close to the sound of the jingler. Jake studied the list of names. Skosha, B.J., Bunkie, Lita, Beki, Herb, Lefty, Heidi, Sissy, Sundance, Nellie, and Dagwood. He smiled. "Well, Dad always wanted me to have friends," he mused. "Now I've got twelve."

Whether Dad knew it or not, *he* was still a problem, and two nights later, as they lingered over Nora's apple pie at the supper table, Win managed to put his finger on a matter that was as touchy as the boil Jake once had on the back of his neck. "Guess your Dad's bound to be proud of this caper you're pulling off, Jake. Isn't every father whose son runs a thousand-mile dog race, huh?"

Jake squirmed and polished up the last few crumbs of pie from his plate. "Yeah, I suppose so," he said slowly. "Except he doesn't know anything about it yet."

Win's blue-beetle eyes squinched shut in dismay. "Omigod. You mean you haven't told your family what you're up to?"

"I didn't know how." Jake groaned and wished he hadn't had a second wedge of pie. It seemed to be fighting in the pit of his stomach with the first one. "I mean, how would it sound to *you?* 'Hi there, folks, this is your suicidal offspring calling to let you know he's taking off on a thousand-mile dog race through the snows of wild Alaska.' They all thought I was a basket case before. What'll they think when I drop *that* news on 'em?"

"But Jake, you can't take off without telling them first," Win said. He rested his fork against his pie plate. "Other-wise it's gonna look like you were trying to spring something on them, like you didn't trust 'em enough to let them know."

Jake rubbed his eyes. Win was only putting into words what he'd known for weeks without being told. "I suppose I better call 'em pretty quick. . . ."

"Like quicker than that, kid. The musher's banquet is only one night away, in case it slipped your mind, and you'll be drawing for a place in the starting chute. You can't afford to wait any longer."

The moment he got Dad on the phone, however, all the old familiar feelings of smallness and clumsiness washed over Jake as if he'd been gone from home only a week, rather than a year. How come he could never act like a person with Dad? Why did he always have to feel like a . . . son? They'd never be equals, that was the problem. He would always be second best. "Dad? Hey, Dad, you remember that kid I told you about? Danny Yumiat?"

"Sure, Jake! Now let me think a minute. He was the one, yes, I think you told me he died in some sort of accident, right?"

Accident. Well, that'd have to be explained later. "Right, Dad. Well, like I told you before, Danny was interested in racing sled dogs. After we got to be friends, I got interested in it, too, and I thought maybe I would . . ."

"You, Jake? You never even used to like Ping-Pong. This doesn't sound quite like you." There was a light, mocking note in Dad's voice.

"Anyway, Dad," Jake went on, determined to break the news, "they have a race up here once a year, and I thought I might enter it with a few friends of mine, Lefty and Herb and B.J., and I wanted to tell you . . ."

"Lefty and Herb and B.J.? Are they nice guys, Jake? Not anything like Bo, I hope."

"They're real neat guys, Dad," Jake assured him, "and not a bit like Bo." Twice a day they eat off tin pie plates and they sleep with their tails curled over their noses, he was tempted to add. Outside, Jake heard a sudden clamor rise up in the dog-lot. He frowned; it wasn't like the dogs to set up a ruckus once they'd been fed. While Dad began to talk about a big new case he was trying, Jake's glance fell on Nora's desk calendar, beside the phone. A red circle had been drawn around Thursday, March fourth.

That's today, Jake realized, and then remembered why it'd been circled: Kamina was due in town to attend the musher's banquet on Friday and to get ready for the start at Mulcahy Park on Saturday. So that's why the dogs were all tuned up. "—and this guy who's going to come up against me is a real Young Turk, Jake," he heard Dad say on the other end of the line, "a hired gun from California, that's what. They didn't want to send a local man up against me. He thinks he's going to face your old man down, Jake, but when I'm through with him . . ."

"Gee, Dad," Jake broke in, "I'm sorry, but I have to go now. Company's coming and I have to go see . . ."

"Company, Jake? More of your friends, I'll bet."

"Only one this time, Dad. There's this girl and she . . ."

"*Girl?* Jake, you don't sound at all like the boy who left Minneapolis a year ago! This girl of yours, what's she like, son?"

Mean and mad and tough as anybody I ever knew, Jake thought of muttering, when Kamina stepped through the door into Win's living room and swung Angus up into her arms. The fur ruff of her parka was frosted with snow, her black bangs and eyelashes glittered with frost crystals, and when she smiled across the room at him, the dimple in her cheek came impudently to life.

"She's pretty, Dad," Jake whispered, surprised, and set the phone back in its cradle. Weird. Until this moment, he'd never even noticed.

Jake made sure he was upstairs and into bed early. It'd been better when he'd thought Kamina was mean, mad, and tough; then she hadn't seemed exactly like a girl. And girls were still aliens from another galaxy. Maybe she'd stay up late, he hoped, talking to Nora and tying more macrame knots, and if he got going early tomorrow, maybe he wouldn't have to face her until tomorrow night at the musher's banquet. But toward midnight, after he'd finally dropped off to sleep, Jake was wakened by an insistent rapping on the door of his room.

"Win?" he croaked hopefully. "That you, Win?"

"No. It's me, Krazy Kate," said a soft voice from the other side of the door.

Jake switched on the dim light beside his bed and pulled the covers up to his chin. "C'mon in," he grumbled. If she had any brains, she would see she wasn't exactly welcome and would get back across the hall where she belonged.

Kamina opened the door and stuck her head around the doorjamb. "Getting your Z's, Outsider?" she asked. An innocent question, Jake thought, but coming from her it somehow had a rude ring.

"Trying to," he answered, "except all of a sudden this place seems like Grand Central Station."

"Sorry," Kamina said in a tone that let Jake know she wasn't at all. "I just wanted to wish you good luck on Saturday, that's all."

"Thanks, I think. You still plan to race my socks off?"

"But of course," Kamina promised sweetly, and stepped into his room. With one long boyish stride she was at the foot of his bed. She seized the low footboard, vaulted over it as impudently as Danny might have, and settled herself cross-legged next to his toes.

Jake stared at her with dismay. "It's late," he croaked again. "You better get some Z's yourself, you know." It used to be a black dog as big as a St. Bernard on the end of my bed, he thought. Now it's a freaky broad with a black braid who refuses to mind her own business.

"You been training like you meant business since I saw you last?" she inquired, not taking the hint.

"Hard as I could. What's it to you?"

"Hey, listen, Outsider—I think you and I got off to a bad start that first day we met, back in Nyotek. I was still so whacked over what'd happened to Danny that I couldn't think straight. Not only about him dying, but dying the way he did. Killing himself and all that. I got nothing against you personally. That's what I'm trying to say, I guess."

Jake pulled Nora's quilt up to his lower lip. She's actually trying to make friends, he realized with astonishment. That was even harder to handle than having her be her customary ornery self. "It's real late; you probably ought to be in bed, too," he suggested as tactfully as he could. She might want to be friends, but Jake was not sure he knew how.

Kamina studied him for a long moment. "Sure, Outsider," she agreed lightly. She hopped off the bed as easily as she'd gotten on it, then turned to face him before she stepped out into the hall. The light behind her outlined her in the doorway but made it impossible for Jake to see her eyes clearly. "Who knows?" she asked softly. "Maybe we'll even see Danny out there." Then the door clicked shut behind her, and she was gone.

See Danny out there? Danny was dead; nobody'd ever see him again. Jake slid down in bed and raked his fingers through his hair. Was it only his imagination, or didn't it feel quite as pale and limp as it used to? One thing for sure, he thought, I can't afford to be a wimp anymore. Or worry that I'm going to run into ghosts on the trail, either. He shut his eyes and silently ticked off the names of the villages he'd soon be passing through. Wasilla . . . Susitna Station . . . Rainy Pass . . . White Mountain. Those names were like rungs on a ladder, a ladder that led north to Nome. One that he was just about ready to climb.

# 9

#### ∵

AT NINE O'CLOCK on Saturday morning, in the
park outside Mulcahy Stadium, more than eight
hundred dogs were howling and yipping and ki-
yiing their eagerness to take to the trail when Jake and
Kamina pulled up after having run their teams in from the
clinic four miles away. The night before they'd sat silently
side by side at the musher's banquet, poking uncomfort-
ably at their roast Cornish game hens, and Jake had been
surprised to realize Kamina felt as out of place as he did
himself. As soon as the meal was over and they'd gotten
their numbers for the starting chute, they'd headed word-
lessly for home.

"With Kamina drawing a twenty-ninth start, and you
getting number thirty-seven, there's no sense either one of
you getting into town at the crack of dawn," had been
Win's opinion on Saturday morning. "It'd only mean a
long hassle of trying to keep your dogs calm while the
other racers steam out ahead of you."

Over the starting chute inside the stadium, Jake could
see a red, white, and blue banner that read "Iditarod Trail
Race: One Thousand and Forty-Nine Miles to Nome." He
watched it ripple and flutter on the clear, blue winter air.
Geez, he thought, astonished, I'm really here! Me, the kid
who didn't even like Ping-Pong or Scout camp. And when

this race is all over a couple of weeks from now, I won't ever be the same again.

Nora and Win were waiting at the Park with Angus, eager to help hold the teams when Jake and Kamina mushed in. Skosha and B.J. were taking things easy, Jake was relieved to see, but Sissy and Sundance acted as if they'd lost their minds, yipping and jumping like poodles in a circus. Jake shot a glance Kamina's way; she hadn't said more than two words all morning, and now her lips were pulled tight across her teeth, making them look as thin and hard as the first time he'd ever seen her. All of her attention seemed to be turned inward, and as soon as they stopped, she went to the head of her gangline, tied Danny's red scarf Apache-style around her forehead, and then sat with her arm looped around Denedi's neck and paid no attention to anyone.

In the bright sunlight Doc's eyes seemed bluer than ever. "Guess I sort of envy you, kid!" he whispered loudly in Jake's ear, then pointed excitedly in the direction of a small, dark man in a maroon parka and mirrored sunglasses. "That's Emmett Jackson. Comes from Ruby, Alaska, and set the race record back in 1975. Ran the trail in thirteen days. He likes dirty weather, sleet storms and winds and all that kind of stuff, because he knows he's got the sort of tough, well-trained dogs who can handle it."

Win gestured again, like a kid at a fair, Jake thought. "And that jasper over there, that's Rich Swedlund. He's placed first three years in a row—now that's the guy to draw to! And behind him there is Annie Betcher, the finest woman driver in the state. Kamina's going to have to go some if she wants to outrace Alaska Annie!"

But to Jake's amazement, when the race was started and Number One was called over the loudspeaker, no one approached the starting gate. Instead, a hush fell across the entire stadium and all heads were bowed for two minutes of silence. "It's in honor of Leonard Sepalla, the original Number One," Win whispered. "He was the first man to bring huskies into Alaska from Siberia and was one of the drivers in the serum run back in 'twenty-five."

Then Number Two was called and the Last Great Race was under way. Departures were made at two-minute intervals, and Jake calculated that his own moment of truth was only about an hour and fifteen minutes away. "You getting butterflies now, Jake?" Win wanted to know. Jake nodded and watched Nora trying to talk to Kamina. His mouth was dry; his palms inside his mittens were wet. Did Dad ever feel this way before a big case? Probably not; he always knew he was going to win.

"Just remember one thing, laddie," Win said. "There's as many reasons to run the Iditarod as there are men and women to run it. Some run it for the money, although it strikes me as a tough way to earn a buck. Then some run it just to be able to say, 'I did it.' " Jake squinted up at Win; the doctor's lashes screened his blue eyes with stiff fringes of red, and the wind from across the stadium ruffled his flame-colored curls.

"And then there's fellas like you, Jake, who run it for reasons they can't even tack a name to. The thing to remember is this: if for some reason you have to scratch the race out there in the boonies, there's no disgrace to it at all. There's no sense taking foolish chances. Emmett Jackson scratched once, and he's one of the best in the business. What counts is you gave it your best shot, okay?"

*Heck, Yumiat, give it your best shot.* Win could not have known those were Danny's words, too. To have them spoken again on this particular morning seemed like a good omen.

"Number Twenty-Nine," came the announcer's voice

over the loudspeaker, and Jake turned in time to see Kamina head toward the starting chute. He wished he'd had the wits to say goodbye or wish her luck or apologize for being testy two nights ago, when she'd just wanted to be friends. As usual he thought about such things after their moment had passed. Fifteen minutes later the voice over the same loudspeaker zeroed in on himself, Number Thirty-Seven. "Another rookie, folks. This time it's Jacob Mathiessen, hailing all the way from Minneapolis." Jake hoped the wink he threw Win's way looked confident. "Me and my little black dog'll just hang in there as long as we can!" he called over his shoulder.

Then Win was far behind him, Nora and Angus, too, their faces absorbed in the faces of the crowd. He was in the chute, made of snow fence and banked high on the outside with hard-packed snow, that would act like a funnel and in a few moments pour him out toward Nome. A pair of race stewards hung onto his gangline, jockeyed him into position in the chute.

Jake firmed his grip on his driving bow. The flag went down and he heard himself holler "H*iiiii*ke!" in a loud, clear, firm voice that didn't sound at all like the one he'd used on the phone to Dad two nights before. He pedaled furiously, Skosha and B.J. leaned hard into their harnesses, and they hit the trail of the thirty-six racers who'd left ahead of them.

The first part of the trail paralleled the streets of Anchorage and was lined with spectators and well-wishers, but their faces dissolved one into the next as Jake steamed toward the Chugach Mountains. The Chugach, so impressive from a distance, were actually low by Alaska standards, being only thirty-five hundred feet in elevation, and Jake crossed their base quickly, close by the trails he and Danny had once practiced on. He passed through the Fort Richardson Military Reservation, then ran for Eagle River, the first checkpoint of the race, fifteen miles away.

At Eagle River, after all racers had checked in, dogs, teams, and drivers were trucked around a poorly frozen area, similar to the one where Danny had drowned, in order to restart the race on the ice of Lake Lucille, near Wasilla. The temperature had been in the twenties when they left Anchorage, and Jake was glad that by the time they reached Lake Lucille it had dropped to ten and a cold wind had risen. A year ago, he thought wryly, I hated weather like this; now that I know it's what makes a team run well, I hate to see it warm! Not that I exactly look forward to temps like they have in the Interior, where Red says the mercury can go off the scale on a thermometer that reads minus one hundred and thirty, Jake thought. Even the dogs might not approve of that.

Jake looked around for Kamina. She must've already gotten a ride to Wasilla, for she was nowhere in sight. After the restart on the ice of Lake Lucille, the next stop would be Knik, another fifteen miles beyond. Knik . . . where Danny's dogs had run with their broken sled after the accident. Accident, Mathiessen? Starting today, you're never going to call it that again, Jake decided. He hung low over his driving bow and fastened his gaze somewhere between Skosha's pricked ears and B.J.'s floppy ones.

But maybe what happened to me and Danny *were* accidents in a way, Jake decided. Maybe life was like a race, and you shouldn't feel embarrassed not to be first or best or a winner all the time. The guy with the mirrored sunglasses, who'd set the record for the Iditarod, *he* didn't always win. Of course, if you had a father who never lost at anything, not even a game of checkers. . . . Jake squinted against the glare of the sun on the snow and shifted his weight when the sled hit a small bump in the trail. For two weeks at least, he wouldn't have time to think about suicides and accidents and fathers who never lost. The arch over Front Street was still a thousand miles away, and mushing under it was the only thing that mattered now.

Eagle River, Wasilla, Knik . . . the first three rungs on the ladder, and it was nearly dark when Jake mushed his team through the tiny village of Knik. Should he try to get as far as Susitna Station? he wondered. Then, in the woods that surrounded Knik, where pieces of Danny's old sled must be buried, Jake saw clustered dots of orange light. Campfires. Some of the other mushers had decided to make camp; he would, too.

"How're you doin', rookie?" came a friendly voice from behind a campfire as Jake passed by. "Okay—I think!" he hollered back. So far the whole thing seemed almost too easy. Everybody had come down on him with stories about the horrors of the trail, from Nora to Red Pulaski to a kid in school whose cousin had run the Iditarod and swore he'd never be crazy enough to do it again. So far, though, it'd been a piece of cake.

Jake passed groups of campers and dogs, then several mushers who'd pulled off to be by themselves. Finally he picked a spot for himself deeper into the woods than any of the others, lashed his sled to a tree with his snub rope, and began to unhitch the team. Each dog shook itself and rolled in the snow. "You guys think it's been a piece of cake, too, don't you?" Jake teased. They were like kids who'd been let out for recess. B.J. was the only one who curled himself into a ball and looked sullen.

After each dog had been staked, Jake cut spruce boughs

for bedding for each one, then unpacked his sled and set up the Coleman stove. He scooped snow, melted it, waited for the water to boil. Within an hour the dogs were eating their rice-and-meat meal, fortified with oil, vitamins, and bone meal, and had curled themselves on their evergreen beds.

"My turn now," Jake told them, then saw that the only one still awake was B.J. The dog's eyes were hard and yellow in the dim light of the twig fire Jake had built while he waited for Nora's chili to warm through in its ziplock container. When it was ready to eat, Jake cupped the bag in a mittened hand and spooned the steaming chili down his gullet. He was half finished when a too familiar voice behind him inquired brusquely, "Well, how'd the first leg go, Outsider?"

Kamina stepped around him into the circle of light cast by the tiny fire. "Not too bad," Jake chirped and hoped he sounded as positive as he felt. "Where'd you camp?" he asked.

"Down the trail a piece. I want to light out first thing in the a.m. Some of the real hot drivers are camped even out beyond me; bet they don't rest more'n a few hours." Kamina scrunched her insulated boots back and forth in the snow. "By tomorrow night you'll really be able to tell the leaders from the middle runners, and the middle runners from the last-in-liners. We have to cross some muskeg tomorrow, y'know, and that'll really help weed out the ones who're making this run just for the heck of it."

Maybe she means me, Jake thought. He poked his spoon toward his chili pouch with more charity than he felt. "You already eaten? I got enough here to share."

"Naw, I already ate." She paused again and Jake knew there was something else she wanted to say. "You know

what was on my mind when we came into these woods?"
she asked finally.

"Same thing that was on mine, I bet," Jake said.
"Danny, right? I guess that's only natural. After all, this is
where..."

"Where they found the sled," Kamina finished for him.
She scuffed her feet in the snow again. "There's a story
some of the Old Ones in certain tribes told about souls.
See, they believed that babies were born without souls,
that they grew up and had to search for the ones that
belonged to them. When a person found a soul, it might
be in the heart of a tree. Or in the eye of a wolf. Or in the
wings of a raven. They took the souls for their own but
when they died, the tree and the wolf and the raven took
them back again."

"Kind of a hard story to swallow, right?" Jake observed.

"Oh, I don't know about that," Kamina answered
slowly. "Sometimes, when I'm out in the woods like this, I
think it might be true. You just never can tell about those
old stories...."

"Kamina, the only thing I know for sure is that Danny *is*
dead. You and I are here to run a race for him, that's all I
know," Jake said, and was startled by the coolness of his
own words. Maybe it was because her talk about souls and
looking for one made him uneasy, he decided.

"Sometimes it's what we can't see or explain that counts
most, Outsider," she replied softly. She stepped quickly
away from the fire, then called out of the darkness to him,
her voice loud and brusque once again, "Don't forget to
take off your socks tonight, either!"

"So you can't race 'em off me in my sleep?"

"Keep 'em on all night and by morning they'll be so
clammy and ugly you won't be able to stand 'em. But if you
take 'em off and throw 'em into the bottom of your sleep-

ing bag, they'll be dry and ready to wear when you get up." Jake listened to her footsteps recede into the Alaska night. She thought she was so smart about everything, even other peoples' socks.

After he'd cleaned up his cooking gear and brushed his teeth with the last half-cupful of warm water, Jake got ready to crawl into his sleeping bag. Skosha was curled in the corner of the tent, and when Jake turned, he saw the blue hound, yellow eyes still wide open, studying him from across the dying fire. Jake crawled back out of the tent, circled the fire, and unsnapped the dog from his stake chain. "I don't care whether you're a loner or not, buddy," he said, "but it behooves me to take good care of both my leaders. From now on you sleep in the tent with Skosha and me." B.J. resisted being pulled into the tent but finally settled himself stiffly on the boughs Jake spread out for him in the corner opposite Skosha.

Jake crawled into his sleeping bag, stretched out, and ran his fingers over his face. Then he remembered he'd forgotten to pack a razor. Not that he had to shave every day, but in two weeks . . . wow, he'd look like some old sourdough just in from his claim for a month's rations. With his index finger he casually explored the scar under his ear. So smooth now, so harmless. He wiggled his toes and realized he still had his socks on. What if Krazy Kate knew what she was talking about? Well, he had two feet and there was a good way to make a scientific comparison with one test foot and one control foot. He reached down and pulled off one sock, smiled into the dark, and hoped she was wrong.

The next morning Jake groaned, stretched, and hauled himself upright out of his sleeping bag. B.J. eyed him suspiciously. Jake grabbed his knit cap and reached down to check the sock experiment. The foot still besocked was, as Kamina had promised, clammy and ugly. The loose sock, at the bottom of the bag, was dry and ready to wear. "Chalk up a point for the competition," he told B.J. wryly, and to his amazement, the blue hound's tail gave a single agreeable thump on the floor of the tent.

Outside it was not quite light, but Jake could tell from the stillness that the surrounding woods were empty. He was the last musher to leave; the others could be as much as two or three hours ahead of him. He fed the team as quickly as he could and decided not to eat himself, although it was a timesaver Doc had warned him against. "You have to keep yourself in as good shape as any member of your team," Win had counseled. "*You* need a healthy team to finish the race; *they* need a healthy driver to finish."

When Jake harnessed the dogs, he could tell they felt as fresh as they had the day before, and as he came out of the woods and headed toward Susitna Station, he could see how neatly the other campsites had been left. No debris was left lying about; all the fires had been doused and the coals spread around in the snow.

In the Susitna River Valley, Jake found himself traversing the muskeg swamp that Kamina had warned him about. As the sky brightened he could see other mushers far in the distance, in a long string like beads on a child's pull-toy, but it was impossible to tell which bead was Kamina. It was also impossible to always avoid the wet, boggy patches of open water in the valley, and the team stepped through such stretches with distaste, hating to get their feet soaked.

Once out of the muskeg and into a patch of alder woods, Jake encouraged the team to lope, then wished he hadn't.

Coming around a tight corner in the trail, he found himself running on top of another musher, whose dogs were badly tangled in the thick, leafless brush. Jake called a frantic "Gee! Gee!" to Skosha and she bent as far to the right as she could, which was not far enough. In a moment his own twelve dogs were piled on top of more dogs than Jake could count.

"Sorry about that, fella," a disgusted-looking stranger groaned. "I got off the trail somehow and was just doubling back when my team kinda crossed over itself. Guess that's what I get for having such a long gangline."

"How many dogs you got?" Jake wondered aloud. "Looks to me like it just snowed dogs here!"

"Twenty," was the reply. "Sometimes, if it's foggy, I can't even see my leaders! But I figure I can drop half the bunch, if I have to, and still have enough of a team left to finish real strong."

Jake snubbed his sled to a tree and set about helping the other musher sort out dogs and lines. "You must be one of the younger guys," the stranger observed. "Don't think we've met. My name's Willie Bauer, and I ran last year, too."

Jake kept his head down. "Name's Mathiessen," he said gruffly, and added nothing about being an Outsider.

After the Bauer team was straightened out, their driver motioned Jake ahead. "I won't hold you up anymore, kid, but thanks for sticking around to give me a hand. I'd have been here twice as long if you hadn't showed up."

Jake mushed ahead, and when the trail rose suddenly in front of him, he jumped off the sled and ran beside it to lighten the load for his team. What was there about the encounter with Willie Bauer that made him feel good? he wondered. Willie Bauer, stranger, had treated him as if

Jake Mathiessen, Outsider, had every right to be on the trail. Practically like I was his equal, Jake realized.

"You're doing okay, rookie," the race steward at Susitna Station remarked as Jake checked through. "You ain't the first, but you ain't the last either, and in a marathon like this one, the middle ain't the worst place to be."

"Has Kamina Yumiat gone through yet?" Jake asked.

"Danny's sis, you mean? Lemme check here. . . ." The steward checked his clipboard. "Yeah, she came through about five o'clock this morning. You know her?"

Jake shook his head. "Not really. I was good friends with her brother, that's all."

"You must be the kid who trained with Danny, right? Geez, it was too bad, what happened to him. Just one of those things, I guess."

"Just one of those things," Jake agreed. "Say, how far are we from Anchorage now?"

"About fifty miles. Skwentna, your next checkpoint, will be another fifty miles. That's where a lot of racers start to drop dogs. Most everybody has at least one dog who'll begin to show signs of not being able to make it all the way to Nome. Some mushers, if it's their first race, hate to drop a dog so early. What they forget is that you can only go as fast as your slowest dog. So if you have to drop old Gus or little Mollie or whomever, don't be afraid to do it early, kid. On account of when you reach Skwentna, you are going to see something that'll make you wonder what you're doing out here at all."

"What's that?" Jake asked, a thrill of fear running down his spine. "Never mind," the steward said, a foxy glint in his eye, "but when you see it, you'll know what I mean."

Jake moved his team off to the side of the trail at Su Station and rested them for an hour in the pale morning sunshine. He stretched out beside the sled himself. You can only go as fast as your slowest dog, the steward had said. It isn't exactly a complicated principle in physics, Jake thought, but how come I never figured that out for myself? He propped himself on one elbow and studied the team. Skosha and B.J. looked great. Sundance was holding his own; Herb and Lefty had plenty of fat to burn. Lita was the only one he really worried about; she only weighed thirty-five pounds, but even she still looked to be in good shape. No, he decided, there's nobody I want to drop yet.

The trail out of Susitna Station had been carved along the Yentna River to Skwentna, a village at the confluence of the Yentna and Skwentna rivers. Occasionally the trail dropped over the river bank or switched around to avoid islands on the river ice, but this was basically an easy stretch and Jake knew that he was making good time. It took nine hours to cover the fifty miles, what with rest stops and snack breaks, and it was growing dark as he approached the sixth checkpoint.

But it was not dark enough yet to make it impossible for him to see what the steward back at Su Station had warned him about: from high points on the river bank that were not screened with trees could be glimpsed a massive blue-and-white wall looming against the darkening Arctic sky. The closer Jake got to Skwentna, the more ominous and impassable that wall looked to be. The easy times are over, kid, a small voice warned him; no more pieces of cake for you. From having studied the map of Alaska, Jake knew that now he had reached the limits of the south-central part of the state, which was bordered by a divide called the Alaska Range. Mt. McKinley, the highest peak in North America, was contained within its mass.

As Jake ogled the blue-and-white wall in the evening

distance, he failed to note that the trail was not well packed and that tree branches or stumps poked blackly through the snow. By the time he caught sight of the stout tree trunk that jutted into the trail, it was too late to holler a command to Skosha. He tried vainly to jump the sled to one side but succeeded only in hitting the trunk at an angle. There was a sickening crunch, and Jake watched his brush bow snap in two. As Red might've said, lemonade-and-ladyfingers time was over.

# 10

THE LOG CABIN HOME of Ben Buono, atop a steep bank above a slough created by the Skwentna River, was the official Skwentna checkpoint. Jake hopped off his sled, shoved it up the bank to ease the dogs' work, and pushed it over the edge onto a broad, flat shelf that was the Buono front yard. The large windows of the house lighted a space across which Jake could see other mushers' teams and gear scattered. It was a congenial spot, well-sheltered, and Jake could understand why it was the place many of the racers chose to spend their mandatory twenty-four-hour layover. He'd hoped to be able to put his own off until he reached McGrath, the eleventh checkpoint, because it marked one-third of the distance to Nome.

"But that busted brush bow might change a lot of things," Jake muttered. Another race steward, clipboard in hand, shook his head at the sight of the brush bow. "Sorry, buddy, I can't check you in until that's been fixed. Race rules, y'know. That way we avoid some guy trying to sneak off without proper equipment—nothing against you personally, you understand."

"No problem," Jake said, although it wasn't exactly the truth. "I got an extra one—got two of 'em, in fact—stuck in my gear somewhere." Once again Win had given good counsel: "Brush bows and stanchions, Jake, they're what you'll bust most often. Better pack spares."

Jake noticed then that the steward was peering at him curiously. "Say, you wouldn't be Mathiessen, would you?"

Jake straightened himself warily. "Yeah, what about it?"

"Somebody's been trying to get hold of you on the phone. Called Buono's twice today, left a number where you could call back."

"Do you know who it was?" The only people who knew where he was were Kamina and the Smalleys. Kamina must be halfway to Nome by now, and why would Win be calling? "Gosh, I don't know, kid. Wasn't me who answered the phone."

Jake unharnessed each dog, staked them close to the sled, and hustled into the Buono cabin; this time the dogs would have to wait a few minutes for their chow. Ben Buono, forty and ample of girth, cheerfully handed Jake a slip of paper with a number scrawled across it. "Don't know who it was, son, but he sure seemed mighty anxious to get hold of you. Maybe you got your first fan, huh?"

Jake stared at the number. It was the number of the phone in the den at home. Dad used it for business, wanted the number different so he could claim it as a tax deduction. Jake dialed it, and when Dad answered his voice seemed small and thin on the other end. It's the distance, Jake decided, that makes him sound so different.

"That you, Jake?"

"Sure, Dad, it's me. What's up?"

"I might ask you the same thing, Jake. Mother and I were watching 'Wide World of Sports' yesterday . . . usually she doesn't watch with me, you know, has her hair appointment on Saturday or Mozart has to be clipped or something . . . anyway, one of the sidelights on the program was news about a race up there where you are. A thousand miles long, they said. Named off some of the rookie racers, too. Jacob Mathiessen, I thought they said. *You,* Jake?"

The warm, moist air in the Buono cabin turned a faucet behind Jake's sinuses and his nose began to run. He dabbed futilely at it with his sleeve. "It's me, all right," he admitted. "Last time we talked, I wanted to tell you about it, but . . ."

"And Lefty and Herb and B.J., Jake—they're *dogs,* aren't they?"

"Yes, actually, they are."

"But you hated to even walk Mozart around the block, Jake."

"I know I did, Dad, but things change, you know. See, I'm sort of doing this for my friend Danny." Jake paused and took a deep breath. "Danny didn't have an accident, Dad, any more than I did. My friend Danny killed himself."

"Oh, lord." The two words were breathy and tired over the wire. "Oh, lord." This time the words were breathier than before.

"But Dad, if it'll make you feel better, I'm not exactly all alone up here. There are fifty-six other racers doing the same thing I am. One of them is that girl I told you about. She's about the same age as me and says she's going to run my socks off." A plump person with rollers in her hair handed Jake a tissue to dab at his nose. He honked vigorously into it. "So don't worry, okay? Everything's going to be all right, Pa." *Pa?* he could hear his father echo. The absurd casualness of the word startled Jake, too.

"Actually, Jake, I've got something to tell you, too. You know that hired gun they brought up here from California? He did what they sent him to do, Jake. He wiped up Nicollet Avenue with your old dad."

"You *lost* a case?"

"Lost it, Jake. Down the tube. Can't even see any way to appeal it."

Jake hesitated. "When this race is over, Dad, why don't you come up here? You've never seen Alaska, right?" And haven't seen your son for a year. "Come up alone; Mom and Mibsie can come afterward. You and I can spend some time together."

"Time together?" Dad echoed the two words as if they were in a foreign language. Then, as he faced one of the wide windows that overlooked the Skwentna checkpoint, Jake saw a weary musher push a golden sled over the edge of the river bank. Behind it was a frazzled, disgusted-looking Kamina Yumiat. "Dad? Listen, Dad, I have to get going now. But soon as I get back to Smalley's I'll call you, okay?" When Jake hung up the phone he realized how many times he'd wanted to talk to Dad, who was always busy. It seemed weird that now *he* was the busy one.

He hurried out of the Buono cabin. Kamina turned when she heard the door slam behind him. The grin she gave him was a tired, abashed one. "I figured for sure you'd be twenty miles ahead of me," Jake marveled. "What held you up?"

"Everything that could, that's what," Kamina sighed. "I had to drop Popcorn at Su Station; he pulled a muscle so bad in his front leg that it looked like a piece of knotted rope under his skin. Hated to lose him, and as if that wasn't bad enough, I took a wrong turn as I came out of the station and it took me a couple hours to turn around and get straightened out again." She squinted shrewdly at Jake's team and his dogs. "But except for that brush bow, I see you got everything you started with. Not too bad for an Outsider."

Jake allowed himself a smile. Coming from her the grudging words were almost complimentary. "How long you plan to stay here?" he wanted to know. "You going to take your twenty-four hour layover here?"

Kamina shook her head. "I've messed up enough. I'll stay four or five hours, then start running again about midnight."

Sounded like a great idea, Jake decided. "That's what I planned to do, too," he lied lightly. "You want to run together awhile? The steward told me that Swedlund and Betcher and Jackson all left Su Station together."

"Sure, why not?" Kamina agreed. Then, as she bent to inspect Denedi's feet, the reason for her agreeableness came to light. "Finger Lake, our next checkpoint, is about forty miles ahead," she muttered, "and then it'll be Tough City, because that's where we start the ascent to Rainy Pass. I've heard horror stories about that part of the trail ever since I can remember, and they say going down the other side into the Rohn Valley is even worse. Maybe it's one time when a little company might be nice."

She reached into her gear and fished out a can of silicone spray. She knelt beside Denedi and carefully sprayed the bottoms of his paws. "What're you doing?" Jake asked.

"His feet were really full of ice balls," Kamina explained. "The silicone will make it harder for the ice to ball up, but you gotta make sure the dog doesn't lick it off his feet and get a bellyache, which might be worse than the ice balls were to start with."

Jake knelt beside her. "Is this one of the Old Ways that are falling faster than feathers off a molting snow goose?" he teased. Kamina aimed the spray can at his head. "Wise guy," she snapped, but the grin she gave him was one of Danny's old sly, forgiving ones.

About ten miles out of Finger Lake, the trail left the Skwentna River and turned up the Happy River Valley, a deep gorge between peaks that rose steeply on either side, to begin its ascent to Rainy Pass. Since they'd left Anchorage, the trail had risen a scant two thousand feet in about two hundred miles, but in the next twenty miles it would rise another two thousand feet. The trail, sometimes only three feet wide, crossed the gorge several times in a maze of switchbacks through heavy stands of spruce and alder.

There'll be no passing here, Jake thought, although he knew that with his degree of skill he was not apt to pass anybody, anywhere. I only aim to go the distance, he reminded himself, his gaze fastened on the glimmer of Kamina's headlamp in the distance. But in spite of reality, in the back of his mind there was always that tiny, unlikely, not-to-be *what if* I place well, *what if* I get my face on TV, *what if* the Mathiessens decide I'm Somebody They Can Be Proud Of, after all.

About two A.M., when the snow began to fall, it did not seem any different to Jake than any other snowfall. In the beginning the flakes were large and light, then they became dry and as fine as cake flour. The stuff made it hard to keep Kamina's headlamp in sight and carpeted the trail with a heavy film that the dogs' feet and the sled runners threw back into the air like dust. The wind picked up, capriciously masking Skosha and B.J. in swirling whiteness, and Kamina vanished altogether. When she finally called back to him, her voice came, disembodied, from the white air.

"Hey, Outsider, you back there someplace?"

"I think so, but where are *you?*" He hollered a loud whoa to the dogs and waited for an answer. When it came it was from only two feet away; Kamina was beside him on the trail, facing the direction from which they'd just come. He watched her brush a hand across her face like someone trying to clear a windshield. "I think what we've got here is a white-out," she informed him.

"A which out?"

"A white-out, wise guy. I'm not sure what causes 'em; somebody told me once that it's a warm layer of air above a cold one. Anyway, the snowflakes don't settle like they're supposed to, just keep flying around, and pretty soon a person can't tell what is earth and what is sky, and it's easy to lose all sense of direction."

"It's really weird," Jake agreed. "Kind of like a fun house at Disneyland."

"Disneyland I wouldn't know about. I only got as far as Seattle, remember."

Jake looked around to get his bearings. The whirling, swirling white air made him feel weightless, as though for the moment gravity had been denied. "Speaking of Seattle," he mused, "what really happened down there? Not that it's any of my business, but did you really take out after some guy with a *ulu?*" Was it the unreality created by the white-out that made him ask a question that might make her mad as a boiled hen?

Kamina leaned across her driving bow and made a face at him. "You're right—it's none of your business." She reached up and pawed the air in front of her again. "But we're crazy to try to go on in this stuff. I think we'd do ourselves a big favor by making camp and taking off again as soon as this settles down."

"There's no way we can pitch a tent on these slopes," Jake objected.

"I saw a stand of spruce a way back; they were on sort of a shelf, not exactly flat, but not as steep as this. I'm gonna head back that way. You go on if you want." She eased her team and sled past him. Then Jake ran to his own leaders and pulled them around so his sled could be mushed down the trail in her wake.

In the spruce grove the snow was deep and powdery, and both teams floundered to a stop. "You want to pitch one tent or two?" Kamina hollered. "Oh, one's enough," Jake heard himself say, as if he made a regular habit of sharing tents with girls on deserted Arctic trails. "Mine's big enough for both of us, providing you don't mind sharing the space with an Outsider and his two lead dogs."

"You set it up," Kamina ordered, "and then chop some boughs for the dogs' beds. I'll get out my stove and we can both cook on it." Giving orders is something that just seems to come naturally to her, he thought as he chopped spruce boughs. By the time he'd made beds for all the dogs, Kamina had fed her team and Jake took his turn cooking for his own. Afterward he hauled some of Nora's chili out of his food bag. "I still got lots of chili and plenty of survival bars," he offered.

"My treat this time, okay?" Kamina countered. "How about some of my mom's stew?" She plopped a plastic pouch into the pot of boiling water and, when it was heated through, poured equal portions onto the tin pie plates Jake held out to her.

The stew was rich and thick and dark, and Jake tasted what he decided was a potato and something else that seemed like a carrot. The meat itself was unusually rich, and its greasiness, which would have offended him in a different situation, now seemed to Jake to taste particularly good.

"What kind of meat is this?" he asked as he swallowed the last chunk and mopped up his gravy with a cold biscuit. "It tastes sort of like pork, but . . ."

"It's beaver," Kamina said matter-of-factly. "Ain't no better way to make good stew than to use beaver meat. My father traps them and sells the pelts, and we save the frozen carcasses. If he has a good year, we can have stew until the weather warms and the whitefish and salmon start to run again. If I had beaver meat to spare, I'd feed it to my team, too. Trouble is, once they've tasted it they won't eat anything else."

Jake felt the warm meal in his belly began to stir. "*Beaver?*" he choked politely. "I guess if I'd known I might not've. . . ." They were such toothsome, hardworking creatures, so cute in cartoons; it seemed obscene to eat one.

"Bothers you, huh, Outsider?" Kamina observed. "If I'd said pork, you'd have thought: swell, give me seconds. *My* people consider beaver as much a delicacy as you think a slab of bacon is. Besides, beaver, with all its fat, is good fuel for your furnace. Your body needs plenty of that, just like the dogs' bodies do; some racers eat butter by the quarter-pound during a race like this. I was right about the socks, wasn't I? Take my word—I'm right about this, too."

After they had fastened their lead dogs to each of the four corners of the tent, Jake and Kamina peeled off their socks and parkas and climbed, fully dressed, into their sleeping bags. Jake's Coleman lantern burned between them. He cupped his hands behind his head. Skosha was

107

already snoring gently in his ear; at his feet B.J. lay curled with wide open, observant yellow eyes. Across the tent, Denedi and his partner, Rab, looked as if they were asleep.

"This is kind of neat," Jake marveled. "Peaceful, too, y'know?" He grinned at the ceiling of the tent, remembering how he'd disliked Scout camp-outs. He lifted himself on one elbow. "Do you know what I mean about peaceful?"

Kamina's dark eyes were squinched shut. "What'd really be peaceful is if you'd hush up and go to sleep."

Outside, Jake could hear the hiss of the fine, dry snow against the roof of the tent. He leaned closer to Kamina and wished she would open her eyes. She had a tiny black mole at the corner of her mouth, he noticed; Mibs used to draw one on her cheek with some kind of cosmetic pencil and called it a beauty mark. "Kamina?" he whispered. "Kamina, don't go to sleep yet. Because I want to tell you why I understand what Danny did."

She squinched her eyes shut even tighter. In the dim light Jake could see a vein throb evenly at her temple. "Can't this wait until daylight?" she asked crossly.

"No, it can't, Kamina. I have to tell you now, before I lose my nerve. See, once I tried to do the same thing Danny did. I shot myself with my great-grandfather's pistol."

She opened her eyes but did not look at him. She stared thoughtfully at the ceiling of the tent. "Was it the same as with Danny? Did the load just get too heavy to carry anymore?"

"The only load I ever had was inside my own head, Kamina. I got the idea my father was unbeatable, that I'd never be his equal. I never told Danny stuff like that. You know why? Because Danny seemed to have everything—

lots of friends, a sport he was good at, girls crazy about him, all that kind of stuff."

Kamina turned, raised her hand, and trailed one finger across his cheek. "Weren't girls ever crazy about you, Outsider?"

"My sister Mibs was the only girl I ever knew very well. Sometimes I wondered if even she liked me." He turned down the lantern; it sputtered and the tent was filled with darkness. Kamina reached for his hand and trapped his fingers in her own.

"You know what I think?" Her voice was soft. "I think maybe there's more than one hour of the wolf. It was probably true that my ancestors really had to worry about wolves, but you and Danny—and me, too—we have to worry about making it out there in the world. It gets scary sometimes."

Jake felt a telltale tingling at the bridge of his nose. Omigod, he thought, I can't start to cry like some stupid jerk just because she actually understands what it's like. He coughed busily, cleared his throat noisily, and left his cool fingers linked with her warm ones. "Know what else?" she asked out of the darkness. "I'm glad you told me, Jake. I've got a feeling maybe now we can really be friends."

"Maybe so," he answered and smiled into the blackness over his head. "Do you realize you just called me Jake for the first time? That's gotta be a good sign!"

# 11
..

**M**ORNING CAME, brilliantly blue and bitterly cold, and when he stared up at the mountain slope that rose at a forty-degree angle in front of him, Jake was glad that neither he nor Kamina had tried to tackle it during the white-out. As soon as they'd fed their teams and eaten a snack themselves, they hitched the dogs up and struggled out of the deep powder snow in their spruce-grove sanctuary. Before they got back onto the trail, another racer mushed past, face invisible behind a frost-rimmed face mask.

"You might as well go first," Jake suggested, "since you've got a better chance of making good time than I do. No sense of me holding you up. See you at Rainy Pass, okay?"

Kamina nodded. The wind was harsher than it'd been the first three days on the trail, and she pulled her face mask down. It was orange, and the openings for eyes, nose, and mouth were stitched in black; she looked like some sort of terrorist or bank robber, Jake thought, not like the girl who'd held his hand in the tent last night. He hated to let go of that other girl and wished he could find the words to tell her so; instead, he watched her get square in the trail, which was corrugated with hard, wind-blown ridges of snow, and in another moment she was on her way.

Clever words escaped him, as usual. The next time he glimpsed Kamina, she was at right angles to him, crossing the ravine on a switchback.

He didn't always bother to call "H*iiiiike!*" to the dogs anymore; both Skosha and B.J. knew that, once in the trail, their only job was to get going and keep going. B.J. pulled with his head held low, pressed urgently into his harness as if he could already see the arch over Front Street. The mutt's just a real mean pulling machine, Jake thought. If Kamina'd ever guessed what a good dog he was, she'd never have parted with him. B.J. had even worked himself up from one tail-thump to two; just the same, his yellow eyes still held their keep-your-distance look. "I won't push you, pooch," Jake muttered under his breath. "We've still got nine hundred miles of togetherness ahead of us, so you can take all the time you want."

After the switchback the trail became so steep Jake had to stop and rest after traveling only forty-five minutes. Kamina was nowhere to be seen. One explanation for that, he knew, was that her team was better trained and probably in better condition than his own, so on the next leg up the slope, he jumped off his sled and ran beside it, anxious to keep the dogs from wearing themselves out any faster than they had to. As he struggled up the mountainside, however, Jake remembered that if *up* to Rainy Pass seemed tough, *down* from Rainy was reputed to be even worse.

"Me, I never had a stomach for rollercoasters," a musher at Arctic Outfitters had groaned, remembering the descent from Rainy Pass. Jake looked up. There's no way, he decided, that going down the other side can be worse than this. He felt his cheeks and forehead under his face mask begin to grow greasy with sweat; he pulled his mask up and unzipped his parka. "Whatever you do, don't get sweat-soaked," Red had warned. "You get those long johns wet, and next thing you know they'll be froze right to the hair on your chest. There's three things to remember on the trail, kid: keep dry, keep rested, keep fed. Skimp on any of the three, and you're just asking for it."

After his third stop of the morning, Jake could finally see Rainy Pass Lodge in the blue-and-white distance. It was nestled on the eastern edge of Puntilla Lake and was flanked by picture-postcard Arctic mountains. By early afternoon he found himself in front of it. It was only the eighth checkpoint out of a total of twenty-six, but he hoped Nora had remembered to pack some clean underwear in his food-drop package, for the stuff he was wearing was beginning to feel as if it had a life of its own.

Kamina's team, obviously well fed, slept soundly in the sun in front of the lodge. Inside, conversation was being carried on quietly, in deference to weary mushers who lay asleep in unrecognizable lumps on the floor of the main room. Jake stepped discreetly among the bodies; none of the lumps was Kamina. To a woman tending a hospitality table nearby he whispered, "Say, have you seen a girl with long black hair?"

"Bet she's downstairs. There's extra sleeping space down there, and that's where several of the racers who came in first went," came the smiling answer. "But as long as you're here, help yourself to some good food that you don't have to cook yourself."

Jake loaded a plate with roast beef, chicken, potato salad, and pickles. Nora's chili was great, but except for beaver stew last night, he'd eaten it twice a day for three days. Outside, the chore of cooking the dogs' food turned out to have been simplified by Nora: not only had she remembered clean underwear, she'd frozen up large ziplock packets of the team's rice-and-meat meal. As soon as Jake got his water boiling, he had only to drop the packets in and heat them through as he'd heated his own stew, and the dogs were ready to eat.

When they finished their meal, he checked each dog carefully. Lita, who'd given him the most worry, still looked all right. B.J., the mean machine, didn't have as much fat on his ribs as would be desirable, and Jake made a mental note to give the blue hound an extra cup of rations each meal in the future. Herb had a paw that looked cracked and sore; he'd need booties when they started up the trail again.

Back in the lodge Jake settled himself in a patch of sun in the main room next to a bearded individual who snored in two-four time. The sun's rays, intensified by the double-paned windows through which they streamed, soaked Jake's shoulders, the back of his neck, the top of his head. It'd be so nice to just crumple over and sleep . . . but he wanted to catch Kamina after she'd finished her rest . . . mustn't go to sleep, Jake. Jake felt his head drop and straightened himself with effort. Don't sleep, Jake, don't. In spite of himself, he did.

He woke with a familiar, anxious feeling of being too late, too slow, too everything. He scrambled to his feet and gathered up his gear. The mushers who'd been laid out like corpses all over the floor had been replaced by new mushers, just off the trail. Jake whirled, looked out the window. Kamina's team was gone. A different lady was putting out more roast beef and another platter of chicken when he asked, trying to keep the dismay out of his voice, "Did you by any chance see a black-haired girl leave a little while ago?"

"Gosh, she's been gone a couple hours, son. Left here by

herself, right behind some mushers who left three in a group. Were the two of you running together?"

"She was only the sister of a buddy," Jake said coolly. "I just wanted to know where she was, that's all."

"About ten or twelve miles ahead of you, that'd be my guess," the woman said as she stacked dinner rolls in a pyramid. "It's about eighteen miles from here to the top of the pass, which is more'n a thousand feet higher than where you're standing. Somebody said the trail was real fast this year; for all I know, your friend might've already started down the other side into the Interior."

With two snack breaks and a stop to put booties on Lefty as well as Herb, it took Jake four hours to reach the top of the pass. It marked the dividing line between the coastal area, where temperatures were usually moderate, and the Interior, where the temperatures would be much more severe, the winds harsher, the trees and vegetation stunted. Having studied Win's elevation map carefully, Jake knew that the trail would now drop a thousand feet in only five and one-half miles. To make matters worse he could now see that the descending trail was made up of hairpin turns and boulders the size of Volkswagens that obstructed the view, plus ten-foot drop-offs that hugged one side or the other of the descent. The ninth checkpoint, the Rohn River Roadhouse, was another eighteen miles away.

Jake rolled his fingers uneasily around his driving bow and wished that Kamina had waited for him. The harsh wind plucked at his face mask, pried at every buttonhole and zipper tooth. Night was falling quickly and the trail was supposed to be the most dangerous in the entire race. But the dogs waited for a command; they looked fresh, in spite of the fact that the trail up to the pass had been rocky and so bare of snow that lichens, green as limes, could be seen underfoot. Well, if the dogs are ready, I guess I am, too, he decided, and started down Rainy Pass toward Rohn River.

Things began to go wrong before he'd gone half a mile. The dogs took the sled around a turn in the trail that was edged by a huge boulder then twisted back on itself, and by the time he got the team stopped, Jake could see that two of the teeth on the brake claw had been broken off, which meant it would be nearly useless in the future. But no way am I sliding down this ice funnel without some way to hold myself back, he thought. He pounded his snow hook into a bank and pawed through his gear until he found two eight-foot-long chains that Win had insisted he pack.

"Wrap these around your runners if by chance you lose your brake," Win had told him. "They'll give you a heck of a rough ride, but at least you'll have a little control when you need it most." Once or twice, even with chains on the runners, Jake had a feeling the team had taken off and was flying down the mountainside. When he bore down on his remnant of brake, sparks were struck on the rock exposed in the trail. He didn't risk hanging a heel over the edge of a runner, however; going at such speeds, he might end up with a broken or sprained ankle. He peered through the falling gloom. If only he'd spy the glow of somebody's headlamp in the distance or hear the yapping of another team!

A new moon, thin as a sickle blade, hovered in a sky crowded with stars and shed enough light so that Jake could see his shadow and the shadow of the team thrown against the wall of snow and ice on his right. He gauged five miles as best he could, then whoaed the team off the trail for a rest. He hooked his snub rope in the crevice of a boulder the size of a child's playhouse, and as he did so, saw a figure rise out of the darkness cast by rocks that were ten or twelve feet distant.

Mushers often encountered moose on the trail, Jake knew—Dall sheep and bear, too, and wild buffalo on the flatlands were not a novelty. But they were not nocturnal creatures. This animal looked like a stray dog. Or a wolf. Jake felt his heart rise in his throat. *We might meet Danny on the trail. . . . Some people find their souls in the heart of a tree or the eye of a wolf,* Kamina had said. Jake wished he'd never listened to such dumb talk. The animal slowly raised its head and Jake could see the golden glitter of its eyes. A moment later he could also see that it was not a wolf, not a full-blooded one, at least; it was Denedi, and behind him came the rest of Kamina's team, pulling the sled Danny had made.

"Kamina?" Jake called. She was nowhere to be seen. "Kamina!" Still there was no answer. The only sound he heard was the wind whining around the rocks and the rattle of his heart hammering in his ears.

Jake stepped forward and reached out to take hold of Denedi's collar. Most sled dogs didn't easily make up to strangers, he realized and supposed that was twice true of part-wolf ones. "Hey, Denedi," he called softly. Denedi allowed him to slip a mittened hand through his collar. "Where's Kamina?" Jake asked, as if the dog had an answer ready for him. Denedi merely settled on his haunches, and the rest of the team did the same. With his hand securely around Denedi's collar, Jake unhooked Kamina's leader from the gangline, threaded his way back to her sled, Denedi still in hand, grabbed the snub rope, and secured it in the crevice of another boulder.

Should I try to fasten a lead rope on Denedi's collar?

Jake wondered. It would mean digging in his gear to find one. He took his hand away from the wolf-dog's collar and patted him gingerly on the shoulder. "Take me to Kamina," he whispered. "Find her for me. . . ." The dog stretched and yawned mightily. Jake looked into those wide-open jaws and was treated to a too close view of inch-long gleaming teeth and a tongue that was pink even in the silver starlight. Then Denedi moved lightly away down the deserted trail. He turned once, gave Jake a long, golden look, and trotted purposefully on.

Jake hurried after. The dog had a long stride, and he soon found himself jogging to keep up. Denedi stopped where the trail dropped off on the left side into a steep, narrow ravine. Just as Jake reached the dog's side, Denedi jumped easily over the edge and vanished into what appeared to be a well of blackness. Jake eased himself into the darkness, slipped, dug his heels into the snow, began to slide, then hit the gully bottom with a bone-jarring thunk.

He sat up and looked around. The ravine wasn't as black as it had seemed from above, and he could discern Denedi, sitting a few feet away. Jake jiggled a loose wire on his headlamp, reattached it to its terminal, then shone a light around the ravine. It was like a prison; white walls rose steeply on either side, and when he shone his light toward Denedi, the wolf-dog stared, unblinking, into its glare.

Jake studied the boulders strewn about. They were smaller than the ones in the trail, and one of them, rather than being roundish in shape, was longer than it was high, and instead of being blanketed with snow, was only lightly dusted with white. Jake moved toward it, touched it with his toe. He bent down. It was Kamina. Out cold. Or dead.

# 12

·:·

KAMINA?" Jake called. "Kamina, can you hear
me?" He'd always wanted to take a girl out. Now
he had hold of a girl, all right, but she was what
was out. Really out. Jake stripped his mitten from his
hand and laid his fingers against her cheek. It was cool
but not yet cold. He grabbed hold of her shoulders and
tried to pull her upright into a sitting position. He pulled
off one of her mittens, too; her fingers were still warm. He
put her mitten back on and peered into her face. He
wished he had something to give her—tea, coffee, water,
anything.

She groaned and stirred like a person waking from a
nap. He expected she'd be angry to be found so helpless,
but she only smiled groggily at him and mumbled,
"What're you doing here, Outsider?"

"Trying to find out what *you're* doing here, Insider," he
answered pointedly. It'd been a lot nicer when she called
him Jake. "I found Denedi up there on the trail. I tied
up the rest of your team, then turned him loose and hoped
he'd take me to you."

Kamina reached down to touch her ankle, and in spite
of her heavy insulated boots, flinched with pain. "I guess I
took a corner too close," she sighed. "I didn't get enough

rest back there at Rohn River. Thought of lashing myself to the driving bow—and the next thing I knew, I was flat on my back in this ravine. Tried to get up once but must've zonked out again." She paused. "Maybe this is what I deserve for lying."

"Lying? Lying about what?"

"My age, that's what. I'm only sixteen. When that race committee finds out, it's gonna be all over for ol' Number Twenty-Nine."

"How'd you figure you could get away with it? I had to show my birth certificate."

"I told 'em the records at Nyotek had been burned. Neither me nor Danny was born in a hospital anyway. At the time it didn't really seem like such a big fib. All I wanted to do, mainly, was take Danny's sled to Nome. Guess in my way I'm even more hung up on gestures than you are, Outsider."

In the silvery light cast by the stars and sickle of moon, Jake saw that Kamina's eyes were glittery with tears of fatigue and disappointment. What'd he do if she started to bawl? he wondered nervously. Mibsie used to cry real easy, and when she did she still managed to look pretty. But as Jake watched, dismayed, Kamina's face seemed to break into sections, like pieces of a puzzle, and when her sobs started, they had the raw, grinding sound of an ice shelf breaking up in the spring. Because he couldn't think of anything else to do, Jake reached out and took hold of her. She cried until she began to hiccup, just like Angus did the time he jumped off the back of the couch and landed in Nora's elephant-ear philodendron beside the door.

It's all because she loved Danny so much, Jake supposed. She's crying for his done-for life, because nothing is going to work out like she wanted it to, because that lie she told is eventually going to catch up with her. He realized that he'd started to rock her back and forth in his arms, just like he'd rocked Angus. What would it be like to love someone the way Kamina loved Danny? Had *he* loved Mibs that way? Maybe not, if love meant it was easy to talk to the other person; when Mibs'd asked him that day why he looked so down in the dumps, he wouldn't tell her anything. Couldn't, it seemed. The next afternoon he was in the emergency room at County Medical.

"Listen, Kamina," he said, feeling that childish tingly sensation at the bridge of his nose again, "we've got to get out of here. Can you stand up?" She nodded, but as soon as he hauled her to her feet, she whimpered and slumped back down. "I can't, Jake. It's my ankle. I think I must've sprained it, maybe even broken it. I can't put my weight on it at all." Bad news about her ankle, that's for sure, Jake thought, but I'm glad she's gone back to calling me Jake again.

He stared up at the embankment he'd slid down on his backside only a few moments ago. It looked like an unscalable white wall. "I can't carry you up there," he acknowledged, "but maybe I can drag you up. . . ." Except that he hadn't brought any extra lines along; the only thing he had to use was his belt. "You got a belt?" he asked suddenly. Kamina blinked. "Yeah, but . . ."

"Take it off. I'll take mine off, too. I'll hook yours around your body and under your arms, then thread mine through it and try to pull you up behind me as if you were in some kind of harness."

"This is all so dumb," Kamina mumbled as she took off her belt.

"Maybe so, but we've got to keep it from getting dangerous," Jake told her. "I've got to get you to the Rohn checkpoint so somebody can take a look at your leg. That's all we have to worry about right now, not what's dumb and what isn't." Except for sending himself to the emergency room, he'd never taken charge of anything before. It felt kind of neat.

Jake hooked his belt under Kamina's arms and buckled it between her shoulder blades, then looped his own through it. He slipped the loop high up over his right shoulder and tried to pull her up the steep bank behind him. He hoisted her six inches the first time, but the top of the bank still loomed over their heads a full ten feet. After several hopeless, grunting tries, he collapsed into the ravine beside her.

"I've got a feeling this particular plan isn't going to work, Kamina," he said. "I might end up breaking your other ankle instead."

"Take Denedi and go back to get my team," she ordered. She can't resist giving one last command, Jake thought wryly. "Unhitch my gangline from the sled bridle. Bring my snow ax down with you, and if you carve some toe-holds in that wall, maybe then the dogs could haul me up."

Jake eyed the smooth alabaster wall. "You might be right about some toe-holds," he admitted, and fished around in the pockets of his parka. No knife, not even a fingernail clipper. "You got a knife?" he asked.

The dried paths of her tears glimmered in the silver light when she turned to look at him. "What do you think?" she asked. She reached into her parka and took out her *ulu*. "Do you think I'd go anywhere without this?" She laid it in his mittened palm.

Jack had seen such knives in the windows of tourist shops but had never held one before. Now, with its wooden handle cupped in his palm, he could understand why the *ulu* was a favorite tool among Alaska natives and bush people. With short, choppy strokes, he began to hack toe-holds in a diagonal path up the wall of hard-packed snow. "By the way," he murmured innocently, "you never got around to telling me what happened in Seattle." He chopped another toe-hold, then another, and waited for her answer.

"Curiosity's killing you, right? Well, this dude stopped me in the aisle of a supermarket, the aisle where they'd shelved the macaroni and stuff like that. Wouldn't let me pass by, the turkey. How about a little kiss from an Indian miss, he asks me. This Indian miss doesn't just give 'em away, I told him, and when he backed me into the spaghetti, I took out my knife. Let me tell you, he disappeared real quick! It wasn't true that I chased him three blocks down the street, though. Somebody must've made up that part. Satisfied, now that you know?"

It was too cold to grin widely, but Jake managed a small, stiff one. "Now that I know the truth, I just won't be scared of you anymore, that's all."

Kamina leaned over and touched him lightly on the knee. "You know something? You're not really as scared as you think you are. Of me or anything else. Give yourself a little credit, Jake." *A little credit, Jake.* The thought had never occurred to him before. Jake gave her another small, pinched grin and began to chop a second set of toe-holds beside the first pair.

"Now curiosity is killing *me*," Kamina observed. "What's that second set for? You've only got two feet."

"For you—you'll use this bottom set, see, so you can favor your bad leg. I'll take the top set, and you can follow along and hang onto me."

"You might be an Outsider, but you're not really the dimmest guy in the world." Part of her will always see me as an Outsider, Jake decided, but it was not something he had time to agonize over. He hoisted her to her feet again, then draped her arm around his shoulder. "So drag that sore leg behind you," he directed, "and let me do most of the work. Ready to go?" She nodded, but after only four steps, Jake lost his balance and they both rolled sideways into the ravine. On the next try they made it only three steps.

Jake began to sweat. He loosened his parka and let down his hood. It's got to be at least ten below zero tonight, he thought, but it might as well be eighty above inside this coat. "Lean your weight into the slope," he suggested on their next try and did the same himself. After four successful steps they rested, leaned their cheeks into the snow wall, then hauled themselves laboriously up four more steps. At last they were able to pull themselves back onto the trail. Kamina rolled onto her back, exhausted, and lay staring into the night sky. "You feel okay?" Jake wanted to know.

"Okay except for one thing," she gasped. "Now you've got to do something else for me."

"Name it." He leaned close to her; the mole beside her lower lip was almost invisible in the starlight.

"Switch sleds with me, okay?" Kamina asked softly. "That way maybe Danny still has a chance to get to Nome. On account of I'm done for, Jake. There's no way I'm going an inch farther than the Rohn River checkpoint, and both of us know it."

"I suppose I can do it if you want me to," he told her, "but there's no guarantee that I'll make it to Nome either, you know."

When she turned toward him, Jake decided that her eyes looked as soft and velvety as the ribbon Mibs had worn around her throat on that long-ago Christmas. "I have a feeling you will, Jake," Kamina told him quietly. Then she raised her head and glanced down the trail. "Hey, where's Denedi?" she asked suddenly. "Didn't he come up with us?" A moment ago her voice had been low and husky; now there was a sharp, thin note of alarm in it.

Jake crawled over to the edge of the trail and looked down the embankment. He saw no dog among the snow-covered boulders at the bottom. Then he peered up the trail to where both teams were tied. No loose dog could be seen. "I think he's waiting for us up there," he lied. By the time he'd helped her back to the sleds, Kamina was in too much pain to ask about Denedi again. Just as well, Jake thought, for there was no sign anywhere of a gray wolf-dog whose sire could drink the wind.

"Looks to me like she's got a fairly serious sprain," the veterinarian at Rohn River told Jake. "Of course, I'm a dog doctor, not a people doctor, but I'd say the young lady is lucky not to've been hurt worse. How long was she lying out there in the cold, anyway?"

Jake shook his head. "I don't know for sure. She'd been gone two hours, maybe longer, by the time I left Rainy Pass. Will she be all right?"

The vet looked sly. "Sure, but this is one Iditarod she'll finish at home, not Nome."

But home and the state of her ankle were not Kamina's main concern. She fidgeted with the blanket that covered her bandaged ankle and did not look any more like a terrorist than Mibsie did. "Has he showed up yet?" she wanted to know.

Jake didn't have to ask who "he" was. "Don't worry," he told her gently, "I bet he'll show up any minute now."

"Maybe not. He's part wolf," she reminded him. "It could be he just reverted, went back to the wild. I've heard of it happening. That's why some racers wouldn't have a wolf-dog cross in their teams no matter how fast he could run." She slumped back against her stack of pillows and Jake could not decide if she looked angry or close to tears. "You got K'enu all packed with your gear?" she asked brusquely, changing the subject.

Jake nodded and ran his hand across his jaw; the stubble of his beard was like fine sandpaper under his fingertips, but since it was as light as his hair, he knew it was still nearly invisible. "Are you sure this is legal, Kamina?" he worried out loud. "I know for sure that the race rules say a person can't trade dogs or add new ones once the race starts. Maybe it's the same with sleds."

Kamina shook her head vigorously. "I've already checked. The rules don't say a word about sleds." Her dark eyes accused him. "*You* were the guy who talked about memorial gestures, but if you've gone and changed your mind, well, then just forget it."

Jake held up five fingers to ward off her next words. "I'll do it, lady, I'll do it," he promised. "And seeing as how my twenty-four hour layover is almost up, I suppose I'd better get ready to go." He rose from the chair beside her makeshift bed, and they studied each other warily.

"So go already," Kamina told him. She rolled the edge of her blanket into a lumpy sausage. "And good luck, too. Really. I mean it." Her face was dark and stern, her voice almost as tough-sounding as the day they'd first met.

Jake hunkered down beside her bed and reached for one of her hands. "Will I see you after the race is over?" he asked.

"Well, I don't plan on taking any more trips."

"Not one back to Seattle?"

"Most especially not one back to Seattle, where girls get mashed into shelves of spaghetti."

Jake wondered if he should lean over quickly and kiss her, like in the movies. No, maybe not; she'd said she didn't give kisses away, and if she chanced to move quickly he might find himself chewing on her ear.

"So go," Kamina urged again. "We never made any promises, remember? Danny was the glue that held us together from the beginning. We decided to run the Iditarod for him. Now you're the only one left who can do it—so go!"

Jake stood, bent quickly, kissed her on the lips. "Keep safe, ol' Number Twenty-Nine," he whispered. Had he just kissed a girl? The fact that he *had* made him feel tall and handsome, and the smile Kamina gave him when he turned in the doorway made Jake wish she'd smile at him the same way a dozen times a day. A girl with dimples like hers ought never to frown.

Jake stopped at Farewell, three hundred miles from Anchorage, long enough to wash and dry his underwear at the local laundromat and take a hot shower at the house that served as unofficial headquarters for the Iditarod mushers who passed through the village. For the first time in five days, racers could prepare their own and their dogs' food in a real kitchen, on a real stove. Talk around the table was limited to what the trail ahead might be like and the possibility of stormy weather.

"South winds around McGrath always mean bad weather, sometimes real dirty stuff," someone muttered. Jake peered at the sky outside; it was only slightly overcast.

He waited for someone else to leave first. When nobody did, he rested five hours, then moved on.

He lost the trail briefly going out of Farewell, retraced his steps, found it again, then covered the next forty miles to Nikolai in the good time of ten hours. Danny's sled must be partly responsible for that speed, Jake decided. He'd hefted it back at Rohn River before he loaded it with his own gear; it was very light, couldn't have weighed more than twenty-eight or thirty pounds. Of course, Danny had taken care to use birch, one of the lightest woods available. He'd spent hours sanding the stanchions and rails until they were no stouter than they absolutely needed to be. Light was what he'd intended K'enu to be.

When he'd taken hold of the top rails to lift the sled, Jake had felt again all the names Kamina had carved there: parents and grandparents and great-grandparents, a brother gone before his time, plus the names of people who'd lived so close in the village they'd seemed the same as family. Jake thought of his own great-grandfather, a man who'd carried a handsome pine four-poster all the way from Denmark, whose old pistol had lain in the attic, unused until he himself had used it. I'm carrying ghosts to Nome, Jake mused, not only Kamina's but my own, too.

When he pitched his tent that evening and slept in it for the first time since sharing it with Kamina and the four lead dogs, Jake realized how much he'd depended on her for tips along the trail, for offhand remarks that made the going easier, for just being there. He had thought he'd been alone all his life, but this aloneness was different. Through the opening in the front of the tent, he could see the night sky blaze with the phosphorescent greens, blues, and yellows of the aurora borealis, or northern lights. Could Kamina see them, too? he wondered. In spite of what she'd said about Danny being the only glue that held them together, maybe she wouldn't mind if he came to Nyotek to see *her*. But that time was a long way off. Meanwhile, he was alone . . . and lonely.

Jake crawled out of his sleeping bag, pulled on his parka, went out to unstake all the dogs and bring them into the tent. Skosha and B.J. were already settled in their customary corners; the other dogs found spots to suit them, curled up, and went to sleep. Jake crawled back into his sleeping bag and, with the soft whuffle of dogs snoring all around him, went soundly to sleep himself.

The trail out of Nikolai was punchy, or had softened during the day, then refrozen at night to make ice as sharp as needles to cut at the dogs' feet. Jake stopped twice, first to put booties on Herb and Lita, then to put booties on all the dogs. As he closed the Velcro fasteners around B.J.'s right ankle, the blue dog leaned over to lick Jake's thumb. "Hey, mutt, maybe you and I are finally learning to be friends, huh?" he asked. But a single, short thank-you lick was all he got; the hound turned his yellow eyes away and kept himself to himself.

Jake checked through McGrath, where he'd originally hoped to take his twenty-four hour layover, then took up the trail along the Kuskokwim River and headed for Ophir, nineteen miles away. Ninety miles beyond Ophir lay the village of Iditarod, the half-way mark of the race. Then there'd only be five hundred miles left to go. *Five hundred!* Jake thought with dismay. *Give yourself credit, Jake*, Kamina had told him, so he did. The facts were that he hadn't had to drop a dog yet and that though he might be traveling at the back of the pack he hadn't had to scratch, either. Nevertheless, Jake noticed that it was harder for both him and the dogs to get going again after a rest break, and once he'd caught himself dozing over his driving bow, just as Kamina had done, too tired to stay fully awake.

Beyond Iditarod the sky began to take on a leaden look, and the horizon was painted with a sullen, sulfur-colored band. The wind started to gust, and soon the trail developed a sugary grain to it. The surveyor's tape that had clearly marked every mile of the trail thus far had been stripped by the wind from the trees and bushes where it'd been tied. A mile out of Iditarod, a musher in a blue parka passed Jake and waved; ten miles later, a pair of mushers, followed by another single, blew by him. I'm falling farther behind, Jake realized; years of experience were standing the other racers in good stead.

"Geez, Mathiessen," Bo had said when he came to the trauma unit, "if I didn't know better I'd say you were some kind of loser. Trying to blow your brains out? With a rusty old gun? Man, that's dumb." His eyes had been hard and embarrassed. Yeah, I was a loser, Jake thought, but you were a user, Bo. Funny, with miles of white, empty Arctic space on all sides of him, Jake could finally see it: Bo *was* a user. Used his women, even used his parents. ("I get a car, Jake, because they're never home. It's a way of paying me off, y'know? It's okay; we don't have anything to talk about anyway.") After that one visit Bo never came back to the trauma unit; when Jake called him, Bo was always too busy to come by. ("You better rest anyway, man, try to get your head screwed back on straight.")

A second pair of mushers passed Jake. Rungs on a ladder, he reminded himself. Don't think about the miles, just think about rungs on a ladder. But miles mattered, too, and he managed the sixty-five to Shageluk in twelve hours. Anvik was twenty-eight miles away; he'd try to improve his time even more on that stretch. But at Shageluk a fifty-foot bank dropped down to the Innoko River, where the trail proceeded to the village of Anvik, and coming down onto the river ice, Jake lost control of the team. Dogs piled over dogs, and when the tangle was sorted out, it was clear that Skosha had broken her right front leg.

She rode back to Shageluk in the dog bag, and the vet confirmed what Jake already knew was true: "Lucky thing it's a simple fracture. I'll splint it and tape it up, but I doubt this pooch'll ever run in another Iditarod. You got another lead dog, I hope? It's a long way to Nome on will power alone."

Jake nodded and cradled Skosha's head in his lap. Her neck ruff was deeper and silkier than ever, but her Arctic-blue eyes drooped sleepily from the effects of the painkiller the vet had given her. Was the space around her compressing and turning black, just like it had around him at County Medical? Jake wondered. "Yes, I've got another leader," Jake said, "and now I guess he's going to get a chance to prove that he's the mean machine I think he is."

At Anvik villagers had laid out a feast of baked moose, caribou, and salmon on hospitality tables spread out in a new log building, the Community Center. Jake staked his team in back of the center, fed them, then went inside to feast himself. Afterward he crept into a corner and slept sitting up. After two hours he struck out for Grayling, eighteen miles upriver. On the way out of town, another musher passed him. This time it was Willie Bauer, whose twenty-dog gangline had been whittled to sixteen. Rungs on a ladder, Jake reminded himself again as Bauer loped by. But at Eagle Slide, sixty-five miles from Grayling, Lita went lame in one shoulder, and Lefty developed a severe case of diarrhea; both dogs had to be dropped. With a nine-dog team, Jake knew climbing the ladder would be even more arduous than before.

Going straight into a hard wind, someone had told Jake, could make even the toughest lead dog decide that the Iditarod race had gone on long enough. But as the team faced into the fifty-mile-an-hour wind that howled around Fox Island Point on the way to Kaltag, B.J. merely lowered his head farther than before, struck out with slim hound legs that chewed up the miles, and cranked along like the mean machine Jake figured him to be. The fierce wind drove ice crystals through Jake's mask to work at his face like razors. His lips were cracked and sore; his eyes felt as if they'd been filled with sand.

From Unalakleet to Shaktoolik, forty miles away, the trail was sheltered behind low coastal hills that faced the Bering Sea. The wind had blown the trail free of snow, and the exposed gravel tore at the P-Tex on Jake's runners. Once past the coastal hills, Jake could see, far to the northwest, shrouded in mist, the southern shore of the Seward Peninsula. Somewhere along that shore was Nome, still nearly three hundred miles away. Then the trail dropped onto the sea ice, which, blown free of snow, was as green as jade.

Toward evening on his fourteenth day in the race, Jake noticed a figure far out on the sea ice. It must be a stray dog from Shaktoolik, he decided. Or maybe it was Denedi; maybe the wolf-dog had tracked him all the way from Rohn River. The dog seemed to be almost keeping pace with him but was so far away Jake could not make out its color. Of course, a weary musher could imagine he saw things that were not really there. Jake blinked, cleared his eyes, looked out on the ice again. Ah, that'd been it; his own tired imagination had put something out there, a ghost dog to match the ghosts' names on Danny's sled.

Out on the ice the temperature dropped to fifteen below zero; the wind picked up and blew so fiercely it filled the buttonholes on the pockets of his parka with plugs as hard as concrete and infiltrated the teeth of the zippered dog bag, leaving a fine, flour-like white dust inside. Whenever he grimaced, Jake felt his raw lips crack and tasted the saltiness of his own blood. The fingers and knuckles on both hands were now swollen and puffy from constant exposure to subzero temperatures; whenever he opened his parka, the rank smell of his own body invaded his nostrils. So when he spied a handmade sign tacked to a post on the outskirts of Koyuk, seventy-two miles from Shaktoolik, that read, "Only Another Hundred and Fifty Miles to Go, Go, GO!" Jake couldn't decide whether to laugh with joy or weep from despair.

Elim, the twenty-third checkpoint, was forty-eight miles from Koyuk. No mushers were resting at Elim when he arrived, and nobody mushed in while he was there. "I reckon you're the last in line, rookie" the steward yawned. "But that's no crime. I heard Rich Swedlund had to scratch at McGrath; at least you're still headed in the right direction."

But just as Jake dropped down through the Kwiktalik Mountains to almost sea level at McKinley Creek and began the push toward Golovin, he was sure he once again saw something tracking him, far off to the left. Had that dog from Shaktoolik somehow gotten lost and attached itself to him as if by an invisible thread? Yet when he squinted hard, he was not quite sure he could see the apparition at all. He tried not looking straight at it, merely trying to keep sight of it from the tail of his eye. It was always there, vague and indistinct as an image seen through waving rolls of heat on a desert, an animal that seemed to be almost the same color as the snowslopes of the Talkeetnas, just like Tanana and Denedi.

At Golovin, Herb finally gave up. He was not dramatic about it, he simply lay down in the snow and refused to go another mile. Jake picked the dog up, carried him to the dog-lot where four other dogs had been dropped, and staked him out. "No hard feelings, mutt," he assured Herb. "You went as far as you could go; that's all I ever wanted you to do." Herb was too tired to offer even one tail-thump in reply. Losing Herb, however, meant that Jake now had an even-numbered team, and someone would have to run in the lead beside B.J. Jake moved Sissy, who'd once run with Skosha, to the front of the gangline.

When they'd passed the White Mountain checkpoint, the trail crossed ten miles of muskeg before it dropped through several shallow hills to the ice of the Topkok River. No sooner had he begun to run on the ice, however, than a storm boiled over the low hills to his left and forced him back to the safety of the river bank. There, in the side of a bank overhung with stunted shrubs and grasses, Jake clawed a snow cave for himself and the dogs, using Kamina's *ulu* and his snow ax.

Jake shoved the dogs ahead of him into the cave, after pounding his snow hook into the bank beside his make-shift door so that the wind wouldn't capture Danny's sled and send it whirling, driverless, across the ice. There would be no hot meal this time; instead, Jake gave the dogs extra snacks and ate three survival bars himself.

He checked his watch; it was only noon. And what day was it? March twenty-fourth? Or maybe he'd only been on the trail sixteen days. . . . He yawned and wondered if he would ever feel rested again. But this was a much different tiredness from that brought on by those pills he'd taken after he got home from the psych unit. This time, his bones were tired, even his toes were tired . . . the pungent odor of wet dogs and his own unwashed body rose steamily around him. He thought for a moment he saw something pass the opening of his cave, then decided it was only the whirling snow. When he slept, Kamina's words trailed in and out of his dreams: "Sometimes, it's what we can't see or can't explain that counts the most, Outsider. . . ."

In the evening, when the storm had abated, Jake crawled out of his cave. The sea ice, as far away as he could see, was covered with a fresh blanket of snow. It was unmarked except for the faint tracks of a solitary animal that had left behind large, dog-like footprints that passed close to the cave entrance, circled Danny's sled twice, then moved far out onto the ice, where they disappeared into the windless, blue-white distance. Jake knelt and inspected the tracks more closely. The edges of the tracks were blurred, as if they'd been made as the storm abated. When he looked out onto the sea ice again, he wasn't sure that, in the falling darkness, he could see any tracks at all. But when he turned his glance to the west he could see, strung like Christmas decorations along the edge of Norton Sound, the lights of Nome.

Jake fed the team again and mushed toward the lights. Even with a two-inch covering of snow, the ice was hard to run on; it was treacherously slick underfoot, and the sled was impossible to steer. After an hour of running, the lights in the distance seemed as far away as ever. Jake hopped off the runners to lighten the load for the dogs and ran beside Danny's sled, one hand on the driving bow. Up ahead, B.J.'s shoulders stuck up sharply through his thin blue coat, and even his hip bones looked knobby.

Slowly, slowly, the lights in the distance grew brighter, larger. Before long Jake could make out figures, cars, the outlines of buildings. Then he was up and off the ice of the Bering Sea and headed down Front Street. The fabled arch was not exactly what he'd had in mind. He'd imagined something like McDonald's Golden Arches, but what he saw was an enormous spruce tree that'd been split lengthwise, propped on stout wooden posts at each end, and had handcarved on its polished surface the message he'd been waiting to read: "The End of the Iditarod Race, 1,049 Miles, Anchorage to Nome."

The siren that was sounded for every musher who finished the race blared for Jake as he passed under the arch. Front Street, which had been choked with well-wishers for the racers who'd arrived earlier, was nearly deserted. Those racers and their greeters had already flown back to Anchorage, where, in another week, the award banquet would be held. Only a half-dozen diehards, determined to see the official end of the race, were on hand to welcome Jake. As they clustered around, a steward with several days' growth of beard and red eyes approached, a clipboard clutched in his mittened fingers.

"Reckon you gotta be Mathiessen," he declared behind a weary yawn, "on account of yours is the only name left on this board. Which also means you're the light on the end of the caboose—you'll get the Red Lantern Award for sure!"

Jake tried to grin in reply. His lips were puffy and

cracked and the taste of his own blood was salty on his tongue. His hands were swollen to twice their size, and there was a festering sore under one broken thumbnail. The little toe on his left foot throbbed from an ulcer the size of a dime, a souvenir of frostbite.

So how come, Jake wondered, I feel as if the sun just came up in my chest, that it's filling this dirty, smelly, busted carcass with something that feels like power? Is it because there's only one Jake now, a guy who can boast the rest of his life that he finished a race that is so brutal he gets an award for being last?

The steward tapped him lightly on the arm, and Jake was startled by the note of dismay in the man's voice. "I hate to mention this, kid, but did you leave a dog out there on the ice?" he asked. "I just saw, well, the darned thing moved off at a dead lope—was headed out to sea, so I couldn't make out for sure exactly what sort of dog it was. But you'll be disqualified if you can't account for each fishburner you started out from Anchorage with."

Alarmed, Jake quickly counted the dogs who lay, exhausted, in the snow around Danny's sled. There were eight weary bodies, so nobody'd gotten lost or run off . . . and as for Lita, Herb, Lefty, and Skosha, they'd been officially dropped, according to race rules. Had Denedi gone wild, as Kamina predicted, and followed his mistress's sled to Nome? Or was that stray dog from Shaktoolik still wandering around out there . . . ?

Jake stared up the street. His tiny crowd of well-wishers had already vanished into the cheery warmth of the cafes and saloons that faced Front Street. He let his gaze turn back to his own tracks as they threaded their way up from the ice of the Bering Sea. The vast ice field itself was sinking swiftly into deep lavender darkness, and nothing at all could be seen on its surface.

He took off his right mitten and rolled his swollen fingers around the driving bow of the sled. The babiche with which Danny'd wrapped the curved wood was slick and cold to Jake's touch. "But I *know* I saw what I saw," the steward complained. "It was a big dog—maybe thirty inches at the shoulder—the size of a wolf, y'know? And the color, it was an odd color, real light gray. Kind of luminous, I'd say."

Then the tired steward lifted his black wool seaman's cap and scratched his head. "Oh, what the heck! We're all tired, and I guess my imagination must've played a trick on me. C'mon, let's take care of your dogs and then hustle up a bath and a bed for you. You look as if you could use both!"

But Jake hesitated a moment longer and scanned the ice field one final time. *Sometimes it's what we can't explain that counts the most,* Kamina had tried to tell him. Had it been Danny, Jake wondered, a boy who'd found his soul in the eye of the wolf, as the Old Ones of a forgotten tribe had promised?

Jake felt the steward pluck impatiently at his sleeve. "Forget it, kid," the man urged. "Like I said, my eyes played me a trick. Only thing that matters now is that you finished the Big I!"

You're right, Jake agreed silently, as a second wave of power filled his chest, his limbs, his head. But maybe, just maybe, my buddy Danny did, too. Then he called softly to the eight weary dogs, coaxed them to their feet, and began to pedal a slim, handmade golden sled named K'enu down the darkening main street of Nome, Alaska.

# 13

· ·

J A K E stepped out of the tent and stretched his arms over his head. It'd stayed so warm during the night he'd slept in only his T-shirt and shorts. Even B.J. had been too warm, had moved outside to sleep under the spruce tree. Now, four months after the Iditarod, only the highest peaks of the Talkeetnas wore a mantle of snow, and the taiga at their base was a sea of lime-green foliage.

B.J. got up from his spot under the tree, stretched, and considered Jake with mild yellow eyes. "You still keep yourself to yourself, don't you, fella?" Jake asked. B.J. answered with a slow, wide yawn and a single tail-thump. It's just your way to be, Jake thought, just like I've got my way to be. B.J. watched attentively, however, as Jake took a can of dog food from his backpack, opened it, mixed it generously with dry pellets. "Here you go, pooch. You won't be needing heavy rations until cold weather comes again, and then only if we decide to race again."

To race or not to race was a decision that didn't have to be made yet, and while B.J. ate, Jake peeled himself an orange and drank a can of Pepsi. Not your average musher's diet, he mused. When he finished, he rearranged his backpack—the canned ham, the extra oranges and apples and candy bars for the children of Nyotek. After B.J. finished drinking out of the nearby creek, Jake hoisted his pack onto his shoulders and turned toward the northwest. Dad had come up four months before for the presentation of the Red Lantern Award. "You couldn't keep me away, Jake," he'd admitted on the phone. "I've been thinking about what you said about spending time together, too." He'd paused, as if unsure how to present his case, then added simply, "I think I'd like that, Jake."

But the man who got off the plane at the Anchorage International Airport didn't seem to be exactly the same one Jake remembered. The hand Dad held out to him was thinner and not as tanned as it used to be. The eyes that had been agate-colored and predatory were merely brown and tired. "You got a nice kid, old buddy," Win had told Dad when they got back to the clinic. "That little black dog he's got is getting to be real trained, too."

"Little black dog?" Dad repeated blankly.

"It's kind of an inside joke, Dad," Jake explained. "I'll tell you all about it later."

"Later" came on the afternoon he piled Dad into the basket of Danny's sled and took him out on one of the old training trails, but the conversation didn't start out being about little black dogs. "I'm thinking of retiring, Jake," Dad said. "Not full retirement, of course. Maybe I'd keep working three days a week. Somehow, you see, I get the feeling I've missed something. You, for instance." The man I'm listening to, Jake thought at the time, doesn't sound exactly like the toughest defense lawyer in the Midwest. "You're all grown up, Jake," Dad had mused on, "and I think I missed most of what went on between kindergarten and today."

Jake slowed the dogs with a loud whoa, hopped off the runners, and squatted beside the sled basket. "If it'll help, Dad, I think I understand what you're trying to say. But we've got tomorrow. Next year. The one after that." Dad had nodded, not quite convinced. He'd hugged his knees and studied the Chugach range as if he'd never seen mountains before. "And of course, it'll all be a lot easier—getting to know one another, I mean—after you come home and start at the University," he'd sighed.

Jake gripped the top rail of Danny's sled and felt the carved names under his fingers. "I'm not coming home, Dad," he'd said quietly, hoping the words wouldn't hurt. "I'm staying here. Win and Nora have already said it's okay with them. Angus said he doesn't mind, either."

The look Dad flashed him was of the old, imperious kind. For a moment his eyes were hard and hawkish. "But Jake—the law practice! It's worth a bundle. I've built a solid reputation on the name *my* father left. All you have to do is step right in and . . ."

"I don't think the law is my bag, Dad," Jake interrupted gently. "I've decided that I want to be a vet."

Then Dad smiled wanly and rested his chin on his bent knees. "Which war, Jake?" he asked ruefully. He'd shrugged and tried to cover his disappointment. "Your mother will be surprised, too," he admitted, "but I think she'll understand." Dad had paused, had studied the mountains again.

"Your mother's changed a lot in the past year, Jake. For a while, after you left, she went to see a shrink. Now the same things don't seem to matter to her—like, if everything matches and all that. She even bought herself some clippers and now she grooms Mozart herself. You'll hardly recognize her when she and Mibs come up to see you in June—she's let her hair go gray, you know."

"Bet she won't have to repaint the living room, either, will she?" Jake smiled.

Dad tried to smile back. "You always had a sense of humor that was a little out of the ordinary, Jake. After I get to know you better, I'll probably even appreciate it. Now, what about that little black dog Win mentioned?"

Jake gave his father a light rabbit punch on the shoulder. "It's a pet I kept in common with Winston Churchill," Jake explained. "See, that's what he called it when he got down in the dumps. Depressed, y'know. He'd just say he was having a bad time with his little black dog." A week later, when Jake said goodbye at the airport, Dad had actually hugged him. Given a little more time, Jake thought, the guy might even learn to like me, just like B.J. did.

Jake had never been to Nyotek in the summertime, and when he stood on what used to be a ten-foot-deep snow ridge, he looked out across a scene that seemed completely unfamiliar. In all directions the earth was covered with a blue blanket of wild lupines, brightened here and there with scarlet fireweed. Below, everyone in the village was busy. A fishwheel turned in the same river that had received the broken sticks from Danny's memorial dance; on wooden racks beside each village home, fish had been split lengthwise and scored diagonally with a knife to hasten the drying process. Later the slabs of dried fish would be stacked in a cache and used to feed both people and dogs during the coming winter.

And walking up the hill to meet him, not sneaking up behind him like a terrorist as she'd done six months ago, came Kamina. She wore blue jeans and a flowered cotton shirt and looked, Jake decided, not a bit less pretty than Mibsie had in her red velour dress on that long-ago Christmas, the last one he'd spent at home. He also noticed that Kamina favored her bad leg and still walked with a slight limp. He touched his shirt pocket; yes, the gift was still there, one of its edges sharp against his breastbone. Kamina waved and began to run lopsidedly up the hill toward him.

"I suppose you've come to say goodbye before heading back to the Outside, Outsider?" she asked in the odd, husky voice that Jake decided he'd almost gotten used to.

"Bad news, Kamina," he confessed and made a long face. "I took a page out of your book. I'm not going anywhere."

"Well, do I have news for you! *I* am!"

Leave it to Kamina, Jake thought. She had a knack for one-upmanship and giving orders. Nevertheless he felt a jolt of surprise and disappointment. "Did you decide to go back to Seattle after all?" he asked.

"Sure did. Didn't Nora tell you about the hard time she gave me when I was in the hospital with this ankle?" Kamina smiled, swooped sideways, picked a spray of lupine, and stuck it behind her left ear. "She told me I wanted to herd my whole village back into the nineteenth century, that I didn't have 'vision.' Vision, shmision—I was so mad I wanted to punch her lights out!" She laughed, picked a second spray of lupine, and stuck it behind her right ear.

Jake stabbed at a clump of fireweed with the toe of his hiking boot. "I think it's a great idea, Kamina," he said. "Maybe down there in Seattle they can even teach you how to talk nice, instead of spouting off like some revolutionary leader." Kamina swung a haymaker in his direction, as Win might've done. "Maybe I *am* a revolutionary leader, Outsider. I can lead 'em forward as well as backward, like Danny wanted to do. But, hey, how about *you?* If you aren't going away, you must be staying. To do what? Run another Big I?"

"Oh, I don't know about that, but after I graduate next year, I'm going to the University at Fairbanks. I'm going to try to be a vet, like Win Smalley."

"*Ehu!* Maybe we can share an office, on account of I've decided to be a medicine woman."

"A medicine woman? That's nineteenth-century stuff, Kamina."

"A nurse, hopeless. That's what I'm going to be." She danced around him, pleased with her joke. Jake touched his shirt pocket; now was the perfect time to lay the present on her, now when she was talking about her new life. "Close your eyes a minute, Kamina, and hold out your hand. I've got something for you."

She grinned and closed her eyes. Jake fished in his pocket for the medallion, then dropped it, together with its chain, into her open palm. He folded her brown fingers over it. "Okay, now you can peek." When she unfolded her fingers, the medallion gleamed in her palm as brightly as the summer sun.

Kamina stopped smiling and didn't seem to know what to say. "Good luck," she read slowly.

"Now turn it over," Jake suggested. "There's something engraved on the back, too."

Obedient for once, Kamina turned the medallion over and read softly, "K'enu."

"I wanted to say good luck in both our languages," Jake explained. "And good luck is what I want for you, Kamina. Now turn around; let me put it on for you." She turned, bent her dark head, and let him fasten the clasp around her neck. In order to do so, Jake had to hold aside the single long, black braid that hung down to her waist. It was as heavy as rope and nearly as thick as his wrist. Then he folded his arms around her shoulders and gave her a quick, inexpert hug.

"I'll come to see you every summer when I get back from Fairbanks," he heard himself say.

Kamina jumped nimbly out of the circle of his arms and turned to lay a finger lightly against his lips. "No promises, okay?" she reminded him gently. "We made a bargain, to try to do something for Danny. We did, too—got his sled all the way to Nome. Maybe that's all we were ever supposed to do together, Jake."

There'd never be a better time to ask her a question that had puzzled him since the race ended. "You never told me, Kamina—did Denedi ever show up at Rohn River?" She seized his hand and pulled him down the slope toward the village. "Sure he did, just like you said he would. Showed his face about an hour after you took off that day. The next morning he and I and all the other dogs were on the plane back to Anchorage. But that was months ago. Now you have to come and meet everyone in the village. They all want to welcome the boy who took K'enu all the way to Nome!"

The next afternoon, after a meal of stewed vegetables, fresh fish, and strong black coffee, Jake packed for his return trip to Anchorage. "I'll go with you as far as the ridge," Kamina whispered as the villagers pressed around with their farewells. Jake shook hands with Danny's father; the old man's eyes were lost in a network of wrinkles as he smiled goodbye. Danny's mother twisted her hands shyly in the folds of her apron when Jake patted her clumsily on the shoulder.

"Oh, I could've told you goodbye back there," Kamina admitted airily, "but I didn't want to embarrass you in front of everybody. Besides, I didn't want to remind my parents of some things they are trying to forget—because I have a present for you, too, and it might make them sad if they saw what it was." Then, when they'd reached the crest of the ridge above Nyotek, Kamina handed him what Jake took to be simply a handsome, hand-sewn wallet made out of caribou hide. "Look inside," Kamina directed impatiently.

The single piece of folded leather opened like a book. Arranged inside, somewhat frayed but still the color of the fireweed that dotted the slope in every direction, was Danny's racing scarf. "I know Danny would like you to have it, Jake. To him, you know, you never really were an Outsider. Somehow I think he knew how much alike the two of you were. It was . . . oh, I guess it was fate, maybe, that you couldn't find out until it was too late."

Jake took the red scarf out of its envelope, looped it around his neck, and remembered Danny's strange, we-share-a-secret glance. As he tied the scarf, his finger grazed the scar under his own ear. Oh, Danny, he thought with a stab of pain, if only you'd waited! Things change, Danny, he wished he'd had the chance to say. I know all about it, he would've added, because I've walked down that road myself.

Kamina watched, satisfied, as he finished tying the scarf around his neck. "There. You don't even look like an Outsider anymore," she said. A small, sly smile shadowed her lips. "Know something else, Jake? I lied about something besides my age." Jake looked at her, puzzled. "Sometimes I do give these away." She leaned forward and placed her lips warmly on his. "On your way now," she urged softly. "You've got a long way to travel before you make camp tonight."

Jake beckoned to B.J., and together they started down the slope. At the bottom he turned and looked back, wondering if Kamina would still be there, silhouetted against the blue summer sky. She was, and hesitated a moment longer, looking down at him. The sun glinted off the medallion she wore around her neck, and the wind had tossed askew the flowers behind her ears. Then she raised both arms high over her head in a clenched-fist, we-did-it-together gesture. Jake raised his own in reply. Then she turned and was gone.

Jake walked, head bent, through the blaze of flowers that carpeted the countryside. He was glad the Yumiats had agreed to let him keep B.J. When Skosha had her pups, they would get the pick of the litter; maybe the whole batch would turn out to have their mother's sweet disposition and their blue sire's ability to eat up the miles. The wind picked up the tail of Danny's scarf, brushing it against Jake's cheek, and he lifted his glance. The mountains to the west that had framed Danny's parents as they hastened home from the stick ceremony six months ago now were shrouded softly in green.

Her parents had been hurrying that night, Kamina had explained, because the hour of the wolf was approaching. Jake smiled to himself. But even Kamina, who liked to call herself a throwback, knew that the beast's real name was fear, that it was as much at home in the aisles of Seattle supermarkets as it was in the wilds of Alaska. Jake wished he'd remembered to tell her that it'd also stalked certain Minnesota suburbs where living rooms were sometimes painted apricot and poodles bore the names of dead Austrian composers.

B.J. waited beside the creek at the bottom of the hill and accepted a single affectionate pat before he moved on. There never would be a satisfying explanation, Jake realized now, for the presence of the phantom that had paced beside him on the ice of the Bering Sea. He paused and squinted into the blue-and-green summer distance.

Had it been Danny, after all? Jake wanted to believe that it had. He hooked his thumbs under the shoulder straps of his pack. The sun was warm on the back of his neck. He knew something else, too; the hour of the wolf would tick his way again, but when it did, he would be ready. Then he called to B.J.

"Hey, pooch! You think we can make it home in one day instead of two?" B.J. gave him a single tail-wag in reply, and Jacob Arthur Mathiessen, once known as Jam, began to hike a little faster.

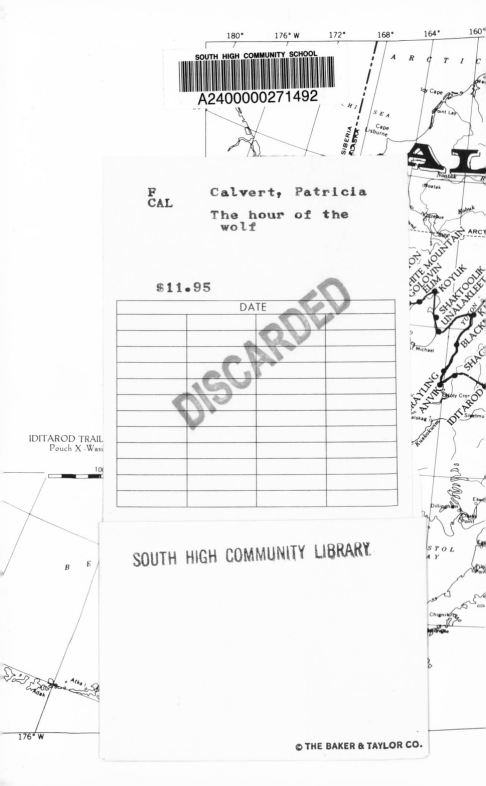

SOUTH HIGH COMMUNITY SCHOOL

A2400000271492

F
CAL

Calvert, Patricia

The hour of the
wolf

$11.95

| DATE | | | |
|---|---|---|---|
| | | | |
| | | | |
| | | | |
| | | | |
| | | | |
| | | | |
| | | | |
| | | | |
| | | | |
| | | | |
| | | | |
| | | | |

DISCARDED

SOUTH HIGH COMMUNITY LIBRARY.

© THE BAKER & TAYLOR CO.

IDITAROD TRAIL
Pouch X · Wasi